Chapter One

Blay thought his little sister Bethany was boring and annoying. *Very* annoying. But he appeared to be the only person who had realised this about her.

Everyone called Bethany, Baby Bee.

3

When Mum wasn't around, Blay called Bethany the Snotty Dribbler, because that's the stuff she was always covered in. In Blay's opinion, they were nothing alike. At seven, he was clearly almost grown up. He was big and strong, brave and cool. Fifteen-month-old Bethany wasn't.

THE SNOTTY DRIBBLER

EFFUA GLEED

ILLUSTRATED BY **KAMALA NAIR**

BLOOMSBURY EDUCATION

LONDON OXFORD NEW YORK NEW DELHI SYDNEY

BLOOMSBURY EDUCATION
Bloomsbury Publishing Plc
50 Bedford Square, London, WC1B 3DP, UK
29 Earlsfort Terrace, Dublin 2, Ireland

BLOOMSBURY, BLOOMSBURY EDUCATION and the Diana logo
are trademarks of Bloomsbury Publishing Plc

First published in Great Britain in 2022 by Bloomsbury Publishing Plc

A catalogue record for this book is available from the British Library

ISBN: PB: 978-1-80199-075-2; ePDF: 978-1-80199-072-1; ePub: 978-1-80199-073-8;
Enhanced ePub: 978-1-80199-074-5

2 4 6 8 10 9 7 5 3 1

Text design by Sarah Malley

Printed and bound in China by Leo Paper Products, Heshan, Guangdong

To find out more about our authors and books visit www.bloomsbury.com
and sign up for our newsletters

He often wondered why nobody else was fed up with finding her snotty dribbles all over everything.

Or how she managed to always start crying just before dinner or as the best cartoons came on TV.

Not to mention how the whole house could tell whenever she'd done a 'you know what' in her nappy!

Their mother simply adored her...
obviously. Their grandparents said
she was sweet enough to eat. And their
neighbours were constantly buying her
gifts that she ignored, preferring to
play with the boxes instead.

There were rare times when Blay thought the Snotty Dribbler was a little bit cute. But he kept that to himself, of course.

As far as Blay was concerned, on the average day, having a baby sister wasn't cool.

Especially when she was eating his homework, rearranging his drawers or fussing with his toes.

Once, he opened his lunch box and found some magnetic letters, his sandwiches rolled up like play dough and only the aftermath of his chocolate chip cookies.

Last weekend, he'd been looking forward to his mates coming over to hang out with him.
But somehow, the Snotty Dribbler just took over the whole afternoon, managing to steal everyone's attention.

No matter how many times Blay tried to get away from his annoying little sister, she loved him to bits and crawled after him wherever he went.

Chapter Two

Eventually, Blay decided that it would be best for them to have some time apart. Just for a week or two. Then his toys and toes wouldn't be snot and dribble-covered. He'd be free of those nappy smells and he could do homework and play his PlayStation in peace.

It would be wonderful. Because being a big brother wasn't always cool.
But how could he make it happen? Where could he go? And who could he stay with? His grandparents were in Ghana at the moment.

All his pocket money, the spare
change in his piggy bank
and last year's birthday
money wouldn't be
enough to get
him there.

Mr and Mrs Mensa from number 53
were both lovely but far too close to
home. So going there wouldn't feel as
if he had actually gone anywhere.

Blay even considered camping in the field behind his school, but he was afraid of the dark. He kept that fact to himself, of course.

That night, Blay lay awake thinking about how he could bring his idea to life.

Before long, he could hear Mum was also up with the Snotty Dribbler, who sounded very irritable and cranky. He got up to see what all the fuss was about. "I'm sorry we woke you Blay. Would you mind holding Bethany for a bit, please?"

"I need to get her some medicine and water," Mum said in a very tired voice. Bethany flopped onto Blay before he could argue, wiping her extra runny nose and tears on his favourite pyjamas. Right then, having a baby sister really wasn't cool.

He was just about to moan at her, when he saw her big brown eyes and little plump face, all hot and bothered. She kept pulling at her left ear and holding him tightly. She cried a strange, exhausted cry.

It was a battle for Mum to get Bethany to take the medicine.

And most of the water ended up on the floor and in Mum's slippers.

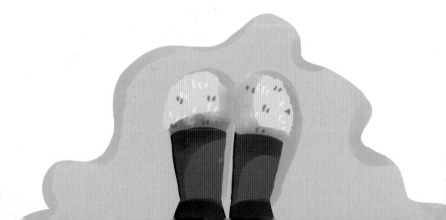

Blay could hardly keep his eyes open,
finally falling asleep on the sofa.
It took a few more hours of
crying, rocking, pacing
up and down with
soft singing, before
Bethany went
back to sleep.

Chapter Three

In the morning, Mum had called Mr
Mensa to take Blay to school. By the
time he arrived, Blay was overtired,
annoyed and didn't have enough time
to finish his breakfast.

School wasn't much fun as
Blay could hardly concentrate
through his tiredness.

He was also a little worried about the
Snotty Dribbler. But he kept that fact
to himself, of course.
After school, Mr Mensa came to take
Blay home.

"Baby Bee still isn't feeling too good, so your mum asked me to bring you home."
Blay said nothing.
As they walked down the hill to the house, Blay noticed an ambulance. He felt a strange uncomfortable feeling in his belly.

Mrs Mensa seemed to appear from nowhere, coming to meet them as they approached.

"What's going on?" asked Blay, catching a glimpse of his mum through the back of the ambulance.
"Your mum said Baby Bee hasn't been herself all day. They are going to the hospital for a little check-up."

Mum beckoned to Blay from the ambulance.

And there was Bethany, pulling at her ear as she lay snuggled up in Mum's arms. A little dribbly smile appearing on her face at the sight of Blay.

"Hello darling. Your sister still isn't feeling well. We just need to let the doctor have a look at her," said Mum, trying to sound cheerful.

Blay sat next to them and took
Bethany's soft little hand as Mum
rubbed her leg.
Bethany whimpered now and again,
but always stopped when Blay pulled
silly faces at her.

Chapter Four

The hospital was lively and full of people. It seemed like there was always a doctor or nurse bustling about, coming by to check on Bethany.

Bethany was crying, wriggling, laughing, sucking her fingers and regularly pulling at Blay.

She smeared snot and dribble on Blay's school uniform, which surprisingly didn't annoy him as much as usual. In fact, it seemed to him as if she needed him which felt nice. But he kept that fact to himself, of course.

A doctor spoke to Mum for a while, saying things that Blay didn't understand. All he knew was that his sister had an infection and would be staying in hospital with Mum for the night. So it looked like Blay and Bethany would finally be apart after all.

He had got what he wanted. So why
did he feel so bad? Had this happened
because of him? If so, he would
definitely have to keep that fact to
himself, of course.

Chapter Five

The Mensas came to join them at the hospital and arranged with Mum to take Blay home and spend the night with him. "Baby Bee will be just fine. Let's get you home. You need some dinner and a good night's sleep," said Mrs Mensa.

Blay didn't want to leave Mum and the Snotty Dribbler, but he also didn't like the smells or sounds in the hospital. He stared at Mum's tired, sad eyes. "Everything will be fine, Mum. Don't worry," he assured her, holding her tightly for a long while.

As Bethany lay sleeping, Blay touched her chubby hand. When he thought Mum wasn't looking, he bent to give her a gentle kiss on her forehead. Mum said nothing but smiled.

"Hurry up and get better, Snotty Dribbler, okay!" he ordered her as he left quickly with the Mensas.

He felt afraid but tried to be strong and brave so Mum wouldn't be worried about him as well. At that moment, being a big brother wasn't cool at all.

"A middle ear infection is quite normal. With some antibiotics and rest, Baby Bee will be just fine so don't you worry alright?" said Mr Mensa.

"Oh, no. I'm not worried." Blay replied holding his head up high.
It helped stop his tears coming down so he didn't have to wipe his eyes in public. His best mate Callum taught him that.

Chapter Six

Back home, the house was quiet... too quiet. There were no hideous nappy smells to greet them as they entered. Blay was able to eat dinner, do his homework and watch TV in peace. And even though he was with the Mensas, he felt alone.

It was strange not having the Snotty Dribbler there to annoy Blay. He felt weird; he was missing her. Blay went to Bethany's cot and took out one of her teddies. But he kept that fact to himself, of course.

As he turned to leave, he saw his PlayStation remote control near her blanket. Before he could moan, he heard Mrs Mensa calling for him.

Mum was on the phone.

"How are you Blay?"

"I'm okay Mum. How's Bethany? Oh, and how are you, too?"

"We're fine darling. The doctors have been to see Bethany a few times."

"They want to keep an eye on her over night but we should be coming home tomorrow as the fever is going down. So don't you worry."

"Oh, no. I wasn't worried at all Mum," he said, letting out a quiet sigh and a secret smile.

After the call, Mr Mensa wanted to talk with Blay for a while.

"You know Blay, being a big brother is a very big job. I am a big brother to five sisters. I hardly got five minutes peace when I was your age."

"Yeah, that's what it's like with the Sno... I mean Bethany. Most of the time, she just gets on my nerves and I wish she'd go away."

"I remember that feeling. But you know, there were times when I really liked having my sisters around."

"And then there were times when I was worried because one of them had a nasty fall and was in pain or one was ill like Baby Bee. But I soon learnt, after having five, that babies fall over or get infections all the time. I think you've been very brave."

"But even if you are brave, you can still be worried about Baby Bee too.

I've learnt that when you're feeling scared or worried, it really helps to share that with someone. And it's even okay to cry too. That doesn't make you any less brave. It shows that you love and care about Baby Bee."

"And I think that makes you a really cool big brother."

Blay's smile was interrupted by a yawn. That night, Blay drifted off into a deep sleep, with a little help from the Snotty Dribbler's fluffiest teddies.

Chapter Seven

There was a delicious breakfast
ready for Blay in the morning, which
was almost as good as Mum's. She
called just before they left for school
to say they would be leaving the
hospital that afternoon.

It was difficult for Blay to focus at school. He kept catching himself smiling whenever the Snotty Dribbler came to mind. He was really missing her. But he kept that to himself, of course.

It felt wonderful hugging Mum again when she opened the front door to Blay and Mr Mensa when they got back from school.

And Blay couldn't wait to get inside
to see his sister. He could hardly get
through the passage before she crawled
over at speed, trying to climb up his leg.

She smothered his trousers with snot
and dribble as expected, but it was ok.
"Bethany... you're home."
Blay exclaimed.

She squealed with delight, smiling a four-tooth smile. She raised her arms and he lifted her up and they held each other close. And there was that 'you know what' smell to welcome him home!

After a nappy change, they ate together and played together. They watched TV together and read together.

Then after a bath, Blay rocked Bethany to sleep and was beginning to nod off himself. As his eyes grew heavier, he whispered in her ear. "I think having you as my baby sister is actually really cool. But we'll keep that to ourselves, of course!"

Twelve Modern Anglo-Welsh Poets

Twelve
Modern
Anglo-Welsh
Poets

edited by
Don Dale-Jones
and Randal Jenkins

University of London
Press Ltd

ISBN 0 340 19517 7 Boards
ISBN 0 340 19518 5 Paper

University of London Press Ltd
St Paul's House, Warwick Lane, London EC4P 4AH

Printed in Great Britain by
Butler & Tanner Ltd
Frome and London

CONTENTS

COPYRIGHT MATERIAL ACKNOWLEDGMENTS

The editors and publishers would like to thank the following for permission to reprint copyright material:

Dr Dannie Abse for twelve poems, 'Epithalamion' first published in *Walking under Water*, 'The Game' and 'Elegy for Dylan Thomas' from *Tenants of the House*, 'The French Master', 'Chalk' and 'Return to Cardiff' from *Poems Golders Green*, 'As I was Saying', 'Pathology of Colours' and 'A Night Out' from *A Small Desperation*, 'Car Journeys: 1. Down the M4', 'Moon Object' and 'Three Street Musicians' from *Funland and Other Poems*, all published by Hutchinson Publishing Group Ltd; George Allen and Unwin Ltd for fourteen poems by Alun Lewis, 'Raiders' Dawn', 'All Day it has Rained', 'The Defeated', 'The Rhondda' and 'The Mountain over Aberdare' from *Raiders' Dawn* and 'Infantry', 'A Welsh Night', 'The Peasants', 'Bivouac', 'The Crucifixion', 'The Mahratta Ghats', 'In Hospital: Poona (1)', 'Song' and 'Goodbye' from *Ha! Ha! Among the Trumpets*; J. M. Dent and Sons Ltd for lines from *Gwalia Deserta* by Idris Davies, and for eleven poems by Dylan Thomas, 'Light breaks where no Sun Shines', 'This Bread I Break', 'The Hand that Signed the Paper', 'And Death shall have no Dominion', 'Once it was the Colour of Saying', 'A Refusal to mourn the Death by Fire, of a Child in London', 'Poem in October', 'The Hunchback in the Park', 'In my Craft or Sullen Art', 'Where Once the Waters of Your Face' and 'I have longed to Move Away', all from *Collected Poems of Dylan Thomas, 1934–52*; Faber and Faber Ltd for twelve poems by Vernon Watkins, 'The Collier', 'Griefs of the Sea' from *Ballad of the Mari Lwyd*, 'Returning to Goleufryn', 'The Feather' from *The Lady with the Unicorn*, 'The Heron', 'A Prayer' from *The Death Bell*, 'A Man with a Field' from *Cypress and Acacia*, 'Waterfalls', 'Wordsworth' from *Affinities*, 'The Guest', 'The Red Lady', 'Strictness of Speech' from *Fidelities*; Mr Raymond Garlick and Gwasg Gomer for 'Dylan Thomas at Tenby', 'Biographical Note', 'Notes for a Picture', 'Winter Walk', 'Consider Kyffin', 'Fourth of May' and 'Personal Statement' from *A Sense of Europe*, and 'Agincourt', 'A Touch of White' and 'Bilingualism' from *A Sense of Time*; Rupert Hart-Davis Ltd for twenty-two poems by R. S. Thomas, 'A Peasant', 'Cynddylan on a Tractor', 'The Hill Farmer Speaks', 'Invasion on the Farm', 'Death of a Peasant', 'Soil', 'Welsh Landscape' and 'Farm Child' from *Song at the Year's Turning*, 'A Blackbird Singing' and 'Iago Prytherch' from *Poetry for Supper*, 'Lore', 'Anniversary', 'Ninetieth Birthday' and 'Here' from *Tares*, 'Sorry' from *The Bread of Truth*, 'For Instance', 'A Welshman at St James' Park' and 'Service' from *Pietá*, 'No' and 'Reservoirs' from *Not that he Brought Flowers*, and 'Cain' and 'The Island' from *H'm*, also for fourteen poems by T. Harri Jones, 'The Pride of the Morning' and 'Critical Encounter' from *The Enemy in the Heart*, 'It is not Fear', 'Sailor' and 'A Promise to my Old Age' from *Songs of a Mad Prince*, 'Adam's Song after Paradise', 'The Beast at the Door' and 'Mr Jones as the Transported Poet' from *The Beast at the Door*, 'Back?', 'Girl Reading John Donne', 'My Grandfather going Blind', 'Welsh Child-hood', 'Builth Wells' and 'Here is the Peace of the Fathers' from *The Colour of Cockcrowing*; Mr Roland Mathias and Gwasg Gomer for 'For an Unmarked Grave', 'Departure in Middle Age', 'Freshwater West Revisited', 'They have not Survived', 'Some Tight-lipped Wave', 'A Letter from Gwyther Street' and 'New Lease' from *Absalom in the Tree*; Mrs Dorothy Morris for twelve poems by her brother, the late Idris Davies, 'I was born in Rhymney', 'Midnight', 'The Ballad of a Bounder', 'William Morris', 'The Angry Summer: 5, 7, 10, 18, 24', 'Dylan Thomas', 'Tonypandy 11' and 'Saunders Lewis'; Mr Leslie Norris and Chatto and Windus Ltd for 'An Evening by the Lake', 'The Ballad of Billy Rose' and 'Gardening Gloves' from *Finding Gold*, 'Water', 'Early Frost', 'Stones' and 'A True Death' from *Ransoms*, and 'Bridges' and 'Stone and Fern' from *Mountains, Polecats and Pheasants*; Mr John Ormond and Christopher Davies Ltd for 'At his Father's Grave', 'My Grandfather and his Apple-tree', 'The Ambush' and 'Cathedral Builders' from *Requiem and Celebration*; Oxford University Press for four poems by John Ormond, 'Salmon', 'The Key', 'Ancient Monuments' and 'Tricephalos' from *Definition of a Waterfall*; Putnam and Co. Ltd for seven poems by Roland Mathias, 'The Flooded Valley', 'Hawk', 'Argyle Street', 'For Warren Davies, Two Years Dead', 'Freshwater West', 'Searching Spring' and 'Craswall' from *The Flooded Valley*; Mr Harri Webb and Gwasg Gomer for 'Synopsis of the Great Welsh Novel', 'Our Budgie', 'The Antennae of the Race', 'Dyffryn Woods', 'Cywydd O Fawl', 'Cilmeri', 'Israel', 'In Memory of Harri Jones' and 'The Stone Face' from *The Green Desert*.

ACKNOWLEDGMENTS

The Directors of University of London Press Limited wish to thank the Welsh Arts Council (Cyngor Celfyddydau Cymru) for its generous financial assistance in the publication of this volume.

The Editors wish to thank, first and foremost, Mr Meic Stephens, Assistant Director for Literature of the Welsh Arts Council, for his encouragement, assistance and advice generously given throughout the preparation of the book. They also thank Mr Raymond Garlick for his enthusiastic support and practical help, Mr J. O. Davies, Senior Librarian, Trinity College, Carmarthen, for the trouble that he has so readily gone to in securing copies of necessary texts, Mr Islwyn Jenkins, for his kind help over the poems of Idris Davies, and Miss Diana Davies for her kindly efficiency and good-humoured guidance and her colleagues at University of London Press for producing such a handsome volume.

Acknowledgment of permission to reprint copyright material in this volume will be found on pages 10 and 11.

INTRODUCTION

This anthology is intended to serve as an introduction to modern Anglo-Welsh poetry. Despite the considerable amount of Anglo-Welsh poetry (and the high quality of some of it) that has been published regularly in magazines, pamphlets and larger collections, the wider reading public in Wales remains barely aware of its English language poetry. There have been at least two recent anthologies, *Welsh Voices* and the excellent *The Lilting House*, but neither was specifically designed for educational use nor for the unprepared reader. By concentrating on twelve poets, we have been able, within the constraints of our declared aim, to give a representative selection of the work of each one, arranged as far as possible in chronological order. We have provided a biographical and critical introduction to each poet (giving the titles and publishers of his work), explanatory notes and a bibliography.

We have been obliged to omit poets (notably Glyn Jones) and especially particular poems that we would have liked to include. Some poets (e.g. W. H. Davies, Edward Thomas, A. G. Prys-Jones) have been excluded by our policy to admit only poets born in the twentieth century. At the other extreme, younger poets have had to be left out because this is not a *contemporary* anthology (though we think that there ought to be such an anthology and there are many poets worthy to figure in it). Emyr Humphreys has excluded himself by his refusal to allow his work to be labelled 'Anglo-Welsh'.

Anglo-Welsh poetry is poetry written in English by Welshmen or by non-Welshmen who have made Wales the basis of their inspiration. It deals with a variety of subjects in a variety of ways, but essentially it illuminates what it means to be a Welshman in the twentieth century. There has been much discussion of the term, and some writers, notably Raymond Garlick (in *An Introduction to Anglo-Welsh Literature*, University of Wales Press 1970, reprinted 1972), have attempted to trace a tradition of such writing that goes back to the fifteenth century.

Professor Gwyn Jones suggests, in *The First Forty Years, Some Notes on Anglo-Welsh Literature* (the W. D. Thomas Memorial Lecture, 1957, published by the University of Wales Press in the same year), that

Anglo-Welsh writing began with Caradoc Evans's publication in 1915 of the collection of short stories entitled *My People*:

> with Caradoc Evans the war-horn was blown, the gauntlet thrown down, the gates of the temple shattered,

and goes on to say that:

> Wales has in the last forty, or even the last twenty, years acquired a literature that will stand comparison with other regional literatures.

Nobody could deny that, after a dismal, amateurish, late Romantic beginning (read through some of the volumes of poetry listed in Brynmor Jones's invaluable *Bibliography of Anglo-Welsh Literature 1900–65*, Wales and Monmouthshire Library Association 1970, if you doubt this), much fine poetry has been written. Dylan Thomas, Vernon Watkins and R. S. Thomas have achieved international reputation and the work begun by *Wales*, edited by Keidrych Rhys and *The Welsh Review*, edited by Gwyn Jones, and by early anthologies such as *Welsh Poets* edited by A. G. Prys-Jones in 1917 and *Modern Welsh Poetry* edited by Keidrych Rhys in 1944 has been consolidated by the founding in 1949 of *Dock Leaves* (which has become *The Anglo-Welsh Review*), by Raymond Garlick and Roland Mathias and the establishment of *Poetry Wales*, founded and until recently edited by Meic Stephens and now under the editorship of Sam Adams and devoted exclusively to Anglo-Welsh poetry and Welsh poetry in translation. These publications gave Anglo-Welsh poets a sense of identity as well as the opportunity to publish their work and reach the wider public necessary for poetic development. Two Welsh publishing houses in particular, Gwasg Gomer, Llandysul, and Christopher Davies, Llandybie, now cater for this public, but the practical, financial help of the Welsh Arts Council has probably been the decisive factor. Wales has never before had so many young poets of quality writing in English.

Modern Anglo-Welsh poetry, like all modern poetry, explores such typical twentieth-century problems as industrialisation and its effects, the erosion of traditional beliefs and long-established patterns of life, war. Like all poetry, it embodies man's responses to love, pain, death – the delight and peril of being human. Certain qualities, however, are characteristic. An important one is identified by Walford Davies in *Dylan Thomas* (University of Wales Press 1972, page 8):

A Welshman, it seems fair to argue, whether he speaks Welsh or not, has ingrained in him a certain view of his art – a kind of collective sense of his responsibility towards form . . . it exists both sides of the Welsh-language barrier, and is itself in turn a barrier against intrusion from other cultures.

Free verse certainly has not been a popular Anglo-Welsh form; to a determined modernist much modern Anglo-Welsh poetry must seem very old-fashioned, especially in its maintenance and development of traditional forms. 'Responsibility towards form' is obvious in the work of Dylan Thomas and John Ormond, but careful craftsmanship is characteristic of virtually every poet in this book. Even a rapid reading will show the poets to be clearly aware of one another and of their responsibility towards the art of poetry.

Twentieth-century English and American poets frequently lament the absence of a tradition to nourish their work and to give them spiritual support, but the survival in Wales of a national culture has, for the most part, kept such agonising out of the work of its poets – far from lamenting the loss of their culture, they draw up battlelines to preserve it against threatening forces from outside. Anglo-Welsh poets have never had to turn away from rural scenes and ways of life – indeed, a sense of (usually rural) place is their most distinctive quality. Wales still offers a rich life to evoke, whether it be that of the industrialised South (though the countryside is never far away from even the most desolate of Idris Davies's valleys), or that of the thinly populated hinterland. Welsh life is frequently portrayed through the typical character: Dai, the miner, in Idris Davies's work; Iago Prytherch, the peasant-farmer, in that of R. S. Thomas. Continuity is maintained through portraits of grandfathers or fathers, specimen occasions such as the big match, the account of feelings aroused by returning to the scenes of childhood. However far the Anglo-Welsh poet may move from Wales, it continues to sustain his poetry – and nostalgia, *hiraeth*, is a characteristic emotion. Harri Jones, settled in Australia, writes from the assurance given by a childhood and youth spent in rural Wales; Dannie Abse, though he has spent much of his life in London and is an eclectic poet, nevertheless returns constantly to his Cardiff inspiration; Dylan Thomas, whose genius in one sense carried him farthest from Wales, demonstrates continually that it is Wales that underwrites his creativity.

A particular quality of language frequently asserts itself, even in

15

poems otherwise unconnected with Wales. Refusing to mourn the death of a London child, Dylan Thomas, as Walford Davies points out, adopts triumphant cadences borrowed from the *hwyl* of the Welsh pulpit. His imagery is also distinctively local:

> And I must enter again the round
> Zion of the water bead
> And the synagogue of the ear of corn.

Many poets fear loss of national identity. Some see Wales as the victim of centuries of English oppression; others are content to stress the national qualities they wish to preserve. Most of the poets have a love/hate relationship with their nation: R. S. Thomas condemns narrow-mindedness (like Caradoc Evans before him) and obsession with the past – 'gnawing the carcass of an old song'. Harri Webb seeks a Maccabeus to lead a new revolution. For some, the nation's greatest glory lies in a past that includes the two Llywelyns, Glyndwr and the archers who won battles at Agincourt and Bosworth. We do not agree with R. S. Thomas that:

> There is no present in Wales,
> And no future.

The present has its comprehensive guarantees in the poetry that we have printed in this volume, as well as in so much that we have had to leave out. If there is a real danger, it is probably in the tendency to narrowness, the failure to look beyond the Welsh pale to the wider perspectives of world literature.

The future will not be as dismal as Idris Davies sometimes feared:

> If all shall be perfect only when every town is under grass,
> And nothing is left of our hearts and tongues after the
>> loud years pass;

nor need it be narrowly preservationist:

> all things pass
> but sea and mountain,
> sand and grass.

Development is assured; its direction is perhaps best pointed by Vernon Watkins:

> Lord, defend us from the peroration
> Silence all that politicians say.
> They who plough us in to make a nation.
> Have not known the vision we obey.

Idris Davies

A Monmouthshire man, born at Rhymney, West Monmouthshire, a town of some seven thousand inhabitants, twenty miles from Cardiff, in 1905. On his mother's side he was of Cardiganshire descent; his father was a miner from Rhymney who became chief winderman at Abertysswg Pit – a highly respected and responsible job. Both parents were Welsh-speaking, as were Idris and Doris, his sister. Though he was to write his poetry in English, he read widely in Welsh literature and had many important Welsh writers – for example Gwenallt Jones, the famous poet, and Saunders Lewis, the dramatist – among his friends. His mother was a devout Baptist and in early life he was influenced by his Uncle Edward, a Calvinistic Methodist.

He refused to try for a scholarship to Grammar School and left elementary school at 14 to work for seven years as a miner at Abertysswg. Here a friend introduced him to the poetry of Shelley and, as 'I Was Born In Rhymney' shows, he first began to discuss political and social problems. After a long period of self-education, during which he was deeply and permanently influenced by the General Strike of 1926 and its consequences, he began to write poetry during a three-year period of unemployment from 1926–9, influenced from the first by Housman.

He attended Loughborough College and Nottingham University where he qualified as a teacher, starting work at a London primary school in 1932. His first poem was accepted by the *Adelphi* literary magazine in 1934. In 1935 he visited Ireland and came under the influence of W. B. Yeats. He met and became friends with Dylan Thomas, had a number of poems published in newspapers and periodicals, and in 1938, on the recommendation of T. S. Eliot, Dent published *Gwalia Deserta*.

In September 1939 he was evacuated, with another teacher and fifty children, to Northamptonshire, where he wrote *The Angry Summer*, published by Faber in 1943. He then taught for a time in the Rhondda

Valley and produced *Tonypandy and Other Poems* (published 1945). He taught for a while at Llandysul, Cardiganshire, before returning to work in London. He became close friends with Gwenallt Jones and read widely in Welsh literature. He returned to the Rhymney Valley in 1947 and published *Selected Poems* in the same year. On 6 April 1953 he died of cancer; his ashes were buried in Rhymney Cemetery.

He did not like to be described as Anglo-Welsh, preferring to consider himself a Welsh poet. There is no doubt that his work is most thoroughly Welsh, in particular of the Wales of the southern industrial valleys and the beautiful countryside that is never very far from their desolation:

> O what will you dream on the mountains, Dai,
> When you walk in the summer day,
> And gaze on the derelict valleys below,
> And the mountains farther away?

('The Angry Summer' 5)

Although much of his poetry emphasises social and political issues, especially those of the 'twenties and 'thirties, his essential concern is always human and emotional – the lives, hopes, aspirations, suffering and death of the ordinary people:

> Your world was narrow and magical
> And dear and dirty and brave
> When you were young, Dai, when you were young!

('Tonypandy' 11)

He was admired by both T. S. Eliot and W. B. Yeats, the two greatest English poets of the twentieth century, and although his poetry is simple, easy to understand at first reading, he has great lyric power. He shows a profound awareness of Welsh landscape and Welsh life. Simplicity is no impediment to deep insight and wide range; it can be the most effective means of demonstrating a concern with the essential issues:

> Then I wonder if beauty demands that men must be put away
> In graves and tombs before her profoundest peace can fill
>   the night and day,
> If all shall be perfect only when every town is under grass,
> And nothing is left of our hearts and tongues after the loud
>   years pass.

('Midnight')

I Was Born in Rhymney

I was born in Rhymney
To a miner and his wife –
On a January morning
I was pulled into this Life.

Among Anglicans and Baptists
And Methodists I grew,
And my childhood had to chew and chance
The creeds of such a crew.

I went to church and chapel
Ere I could understand
That Apollo rules the heavens
And Mammon rules the land.

And I woke on many mornings
In a little oblong room,
And saw the frown of Spurgeon:
'Beware, my boy, of doom.'

I lost my native language
For the one the Saxon spake
By going to school by order
For education's sake.

I learnt the use of decimals,
And where to place the dot,
Four or five lines from Shakespeare
And twelve from Walter Scott.

I learnt a little grammar,
And some geography,
Was frightened of perspective,
And detested poetry.

In a land of narrow valleys,
And Solemn Sabbath Days,
And collieries and choirs,
I learnt my people's ways.

On one February morning,
Unwillingly I went
To crawl in moleskin trousers
Beneath the rocks of Gwent.

And a chubby little collier
Grew fat on sweat and dust,
And listened to heated arguments
On God and Marx and lust.

MacDonald was my hero,
The man who seemed inspired,
The leader with a vision,
Whose soul could not be hired!

I quoted from his speeches
In the coalface to my friends –
But I lived to see him selling
Great dreams for little ends.

And there were strikes and lock-outs
And meetings in the Square,
When Cook and Smith and Bevan
Electrified the air.

But the greatest of our battles
We lost in '26
Through treachery and lying,
And Baldwin's box of tricks.

And I walked my native hillsides
In sunshine and in rain,
And learnt the poet's language
To ease me of my pain.

But always home to Rhymney
From wandering I came,
Back to the long and lonely
Self-tuition game.

Back to the lonely evenings
Of triumph and despair
In a little room in Rhymney
With a hint of mountain air.

At last I went to college,
To the city on the Trent,
In the land of D. H. Lawrence
And his savage Testament.

And lecture followed lecture
In the college by the lake,
And some were sweet to swallow,
And some were hard to take.

I went to Sherwood Forest
To look for Robin Hood,
But little tawdry villas
Were where the oaks once stood.

And I heard the ghost of Lawrence
Raging in the night
Against the thumbs of Progress
That botched the land with blight.

In little rooms in London
The poetry of Yeats
Was my fire and my fountain –
And the fury of my mates.

I found cherries in Jane Austen
And grapes in Hemingway,
And truth more strange than fiction
In the streets of Holloway.

And da Vinci and El Greco
And Turner and Cézanne,
They proved to me the splendour
And divinity of man.

I studied Marx and Engels,
And put Berkeley's theme aside,
And listened to the orators
Who yelled and cooed and cried.

To Castle Street Baptist Chapel
Like the prodigal son I went
To hear the hymns of childhood
And dream of a boy in Gwent.

To dream of far-off Sundays
When for me the sun would shine
On the broken hills of Rhymney
And the palms of Palestine.

I saw some royal weddings
And a Silver Jubilee,
And a coloured Coronation,
And a King who crossed the sea.

And in the outer suburbs
I heard in the evening rain
The cry of Freud the prophet
On love and guilt and pain.

And on the roads arterial,
When London died away,
The poets of the Thirties
Were singing of decay.

And I saw folk digging trenches
In 1938,
In the dismal autumn drizzle
When all things seemed too late.

And Chamberlain went to Munich,
An umbrella at his side,
And London lost her laughter
And almost lost her pride.

And the world is black with battle
In 1943,
And the hymn of hate triumphant
And loud from sea to sea.

And in this time of tumult
I can only hope and cry
That season shall follow season
And beauty shall not die.

Autumn, 1943

Midnight

When the moon is full over Rhymney and the hillsides are silver-grey
And the old and the young are sleeping, and the scars of the
  common day
Are lost in the haze, I open the small window and stare
At the forms of the sleeping town, so still, so strangely fair.

Then I wonder if beauty demands that men must be put away
In graves and tombs before her profoundest peace can fill the
  night and day,
If all shall be perfect only when every town is under grass,
And nothing is left of our hearts and tongues after the loud
  years pass.

The Ballad of a Bounder

He addressed great congregations
 And rolled his tongue with grease,
And his belly always flourished,
 In time of war or peace.

He would talk of distant comrades
 And brothers o'er the sea,
And snarl above his liquor
 About neighbours two or three.

He knew a lot about public money –
 More than he liked to say –
And sometimes sat with the paupers
 To increase his Extra pay.

He could quote from Martin Tupper
 And Wilhelmina Stitch,
And creep from chapel to bargain
 With the likeliest local bitch.

He could swindle and squeal and snivel
 And cheat and chant and pray,
And retreat like a famous general
 When Truth would bar his way.

But God grew sick and tired
   Of such a godly soul,
And sent down Death to gather
   His body to a hole.

But before he died, the Bounder
   Said: 'My children, be at peace;
I know *I* am going to heaven,
   So rub my tongue with grease.'

Gwalia Deserta XII

There's a concert in the village to buy us boots and bread,
There's a service in the chapel to make us meek and mild,
And in the valley town the draper's shop is shut.
The brown dogs snap at the stranger in silk,
And the winter ponies nose the buckets in the street.
The 'Miners' Arms' is quiet, the barman half afraid,
And the heroes of newspaper columns on explosion day
Are nearly tired of being proud.
But the widow on the hillside remembers a bitterer day,
The rap at the door and the corpse and the crowd,
And the parson's powerless words.
And her daughters are in London serving dinner to my lord,
And her single son, so quiet, broods on his luck in the queue.

Gwalia Deserta XIII

The northern slopes are clouded
   And Rhymney streets are wet,
The winds sweep down from the mountains
   And night has cast her net.

The ghosts of a thousand miners
   Walk back to the streets again,
And the winds wail in the darkness,
   And Rhymney sighs in the rain.

Gwalia Deserta XX

O where are our fathers, O brothers of mine?
By the graves of *their* fathers, or awaiting a sign.
The Welsh skies are sullen, and the stars are all dim,
And the dragon of Glyndwr is bruised in the limb.
The brown earth is waiting for brothers of mine
And our mothers are hanging the shrouds on the line.
The deacons are groaning and the sheep-dogs are thin
And Dai is in London drinking tea from a tin.

Gwalia Deserta XXII

I stood in the ruins of Dowlais
And sighed for the lovers destroyed
And the landscape of Gwalia stained for all time
By the bloody hands of progress.
I saw the ghosts of the slaves of The Successful Century
Marching on the ridges of the sunset
And wandering among derelict furnaces,
And they had not forgotten their humiliation,
For their mouths were full of curses.
And I cried aloud, O what shall I do for my fathers
And the land of my fathers?
But they cursed and cursed and would not answer
For they could not forget their humiliation.

William Morris

Because the mind is growing cold,
A slave that bends to the God of Gold,
We have no time to learn your lay,
Sweet singer of an idle day.

We have great problems and great pains
And gas-mask drills and aeroplanes;
We would not understand your way,
Sweet singer of an idle day.

We have no frenzy in the heart,
We play a mean mechanic part –
You would not understand our way,
Sweet singer of an idle day.

We honour dolts in racing cars
And dirty dogs and talkie stars;
Our fields are brown, our children grey,
O singer of an idle day!

The Angry Summer – A poem of 1926   5

What will you do with your shovel, Dai,
And your pick and your sledge and your spike,
And what will you do with your leisure, man,
Now that you're out on strike?

What will you do for your butter, Dai,
And your bread and your cheese and your fags,
And how will you pay for a dress for the wife,
And shall your children go in rags?

You have been, in your time, a hero, Dai,
And they wrote of your pluck in the press,
And now you have fallen on evil days,
And who will be there to bless?

And how will you stand with your honesty, Dai,
When the land is full of lies,
And how will you curb your anger, man,
When your natural patience dies?

O what will you dream on the mountains, Dai,
When you walk in the summer day,
And gaze on the derelict valleys below,
And the mountains farther away?

And how will the heart within you, Dai,
Respond to the distant sea,
And the dream that is born in the blaze of the sun,
And the vision of victory?

The Angry Summer   7

Mrs Evans *fach*, you want butter again.
How will you pay for it now, little woman
With your husband out on strike, and full
Of the fiery language? Ay, I know him,
His head is full of fire and brimstone
And a lot of palaver about communism,
And me, little Dan the Grocer
Depending so much on private enterprise.

What, depending on the miners and their
Money too? O yes, in a way, Mrs Evans,
Yes, in a way I do, mind you.
Come tomorrow, little woman, and I'll tell you then
What I have decided overnight.
Go home now and tell that rash red husband of yours
That your grocer cannot afford to go on strike
Or what would happen to the butter from Carmarthen?
Good day for now, Mrs Evans *fach*.

The Angry Summer   10

High summer on the mountains
And on the clover leas,
And on the local sidings,
And on the rhubarb leaves.

Brass bands in all the valleys
Blaring defiant tunes,
Crowds, acclaiming carnival,
Prize pigs and wooden spoons.

Dust on shabby hedgerows
Behind the colliery wall,
Dust on rail and girder
And tram and prop and all.

High summer on the slag heaps
And on polluted streams,
And old men in the morning
Telling the town their dreams.

The Angry Summer   18

Man alive, what a belly you've got!
You'll take all the serge in my little shop.
Stand still for a minute, now, and I'll get your waist.
Man alive, what a belly you've got!
Oh, I know it's only a striker's pay you get,
But don't misunderstand me, Hywel *bach*;
I depend for my bread on working men
And I am only a working man myself
Just Shinkin Rees the little tailor,
Proud of my work and the people I serve;
And I wouldn't deny you a suit for all the gold in the world.
Just pay me a little each week, Hywel *bach*,
And I am your tailor as long as you live,
Shinkin Rees your friend and your tailor,
Proud to serve you, and your dear old father before you.
But man alive, what a belly you've got!

The Angry Summer   24

Cow-parsley and hawthorn blossom
And a cottage among trees,
A thrush and a skylark singing,
And a gipsy lying at ease.

Roses in gentlemen's gardens
Smile as we pass by the way,
And the swans of my lord are sleeping
Out of the heat of the day.

And here we come tramping and singing
Out of the valleys of strife,
Into the sunlit cornlands,
Begging the bread of life.

Dylan Thomas

He saw the sun play ball in Swansea Bay,
He heard the moon crack jokes above the new-mown hay,
And stars and seas and winds to him would sing and say:
Carve words like jewels for a summer day.

Tonypandy 11

When you were young, Dai, when you were young!
The Saturday mornings of childhood
With childish dreams and adventures
Among the black tips by the river,
And the rough grass and the nettles
Behind the colliery yard, the stone-throwing
Battles between the ragged boys,
The fascination of the railway cutting
On dusty summer afternoons,

And the winter night and its street-lamps
And the first pranks of love,
And the deep warm sleep
In grandmother's chapel pew
On stodgy Sunday evenings,
And the buttercup-field you sometimes noticed
Behind the farthest street, the magical field
That only the heart could see,
The heart and rarely the boyish eye,
And the pride you had in your father's
Loins and shoulders when he bent
Between the tub and the fire,
And the days you counted, counted, counted,
Before you should work in the mine.
You never, never cursed your luck
Or desired to see another town or valley,
Or know any other men and women
Than those of the streets around
The street where you were born.
Your world was narrow and magical
And dear and dirty and brave
When you were young, Dai, when you were young!

Saunders Lewis

Though some may cavil at his creed
    And others mock his Celtic ire,
No Welshman loyal to his breed
    Forgets this prophet dared the fire,
And roused his land by word and deed
    Against Philistia and her mire.

Vernon Watkins

Vernon Phillips Watkins was born on 27 June 1906 in Swansea. He came of a Nonconformist family and was, as his poetry shows, a deeply religious man. He was educated at Repton at a time when Dr Fisher, later Archbishop of Canterbury, was Headmaster, and at Magdalene College, Cambridge. Having obtained his education outside Wales, he chose to spend the rest of his working and creative life in Swansea and on the Gower peninsula. Entering Lloyds Bank in 1925, he worked there until his retirement (apart from the years 1941–6, when he served in the R.A.F.). He was a close friend of the other famous Swansea poet, Dylan Thomas, and their published correspondence which began in 1936 reveals much that is important and interesting about both poets. Vernon Watkins chose to lead a placid, uneventful life devoted to his family (he married Gwendoline (Gwen) Davies in 1944 and they had four sons and a daughter), his many friends and the writing of poetry. His poems began to be published in the late 'thirties, especially in *Wales* and *Life and Letters Today*, and Faber published his first volume, *Ballad of the Mari Lwyd and Other Poems*, in 1941. In 1945 *The Lamp and the Veil* was published and in 1948 *The Lady with the Unicorn*. By 1951 he had established an international reputation and he was elected Fellow of the Royal Society of Literature. Volumes of poetry continued to appear regularly: *The Death Bell* in 1954, *Cypress and Acacia* in 1959 and *Affinities* in 1962. He died in 1967 while on a visit to the U.S.A. and *Fidelities* was published posthumously in 1968.

In character he was a quiet, shy man, introspective, sensitive, and, in practical matters, somewhat absent-minded. Nevertheless, his delightful sense of humour made him a popular lecturer and speaker and he was also a fine reader of poetry. He particularly admired the work of W. B. Yeats, whom he knew and described as the supreme lyric poet of the twentieth century. Yeats's influence can be seen in his work – compare, for example, 'A Prayer' with Yeats's 'A Prayer for My Daughter'.

As a poet he was painstaking and careful, writing many rough drafts before he was satisfied that the poem was complete. In this he resembles both his friend, Dylan Thomas, and his master, W. B. Yeats. His poetry is full of fine descriptions of the natural scene, especially that of the Gower:

> The cliff's crossed paths lay silvered with slug tracks
> Where webs of hanging raindrops caught the sun . . .
>
> ('The Guest')

Though he also portrays the wider world of Wales, for example in 'Waterfalls'. He is not, however, content merely to give a picture; he uses such material to interpret those themes of life and death, time and eternity, which deeply occupy him:

> For the sea turns whose every drop is counted
> And the sand turns whose every grain a holy hour-glass holds.
>
> ('Griefs of the Sea')

'The Collier', an early poem which superficially resembles the work of Idris Davies, is in fact a profound and disturbing religious allegory; 'Returning to Goleufryn', though full of memorably real description, is an exploration of the poet's lost youth that resembles Dylan Thomas's 'Poem in October'. Vernon Watkins never forces his views upon his reader: the poetry is beautifully written and works unobtrusively. The poet himself suggests:

> They who justify themselves are vile.
>
> ('Strictness of Speech')

His own justification, if he needs one, lies in his profound exploration of eternal issues:

> Unless I make that melody,
> How can the dead have rest?
>
> ('The Feather')

The Collier

When I was born on Amman hill
A dark bird crossed the sun.
Sharp on the floor the shadow fell;
I was the youngest son.

And when I went to the County School
I worked in a shaft of light.
In the wood of the desk I cut my name:
Dai for Dynamite.

The tall black hills my brothers stood;
Their lessons all were done.
From the door of the school when I ran out
They frowned to watch me run.

The slow grey bells they rung a chime
Surly with grief or age.
Clever or clumsy, lad or lout,
All would look for a wage.

I learnt the valley flowers' names
And the rough bark knew my knees.
I brought home trout from the river
And spotted eggs from the trees.

A coloured coat I was given to wear
Where the lights of the rough land shone.
Still jealous of my favour
The tall black hills looked on.

They dipped my coat in the blood of a kid
And they cast me down a pit,
And although I crossed with strangers
There was no way up from it.

Soon as I went from the County School
I worked in a shaft. Said Jim,
'You will get your chain of gold, my lad,
But not for a likely time.'

And one said, 'Jack was not raised up
When the wind blew out the light
Though he interpreted their dreams
And guessed their fears by night.'

And Tom, he shivered his leper's lamp
For the stain that round him grew;
And I heard mouths pray in the after-damp
When the picks would not break through.

They changed words there in darkness
And still through my head they run,
And white on my limbs is the linen sheet
And gold on my neck the sun.

Griefs of the Sea

It is fitting to mourn dead sailors,
To crown the sea with some wild wreath of foam
On some steep promontory, some cornercliff of Wales
Though the deaf wave hear nothing.

It is fitting to fling off clothing,
To enter the sea with plunge of seawreaths white
Broken by limbs that love the waters, fear the stars,
Though the blind wave grope under eyes that see, limbs that wonder,
Though the blind wave grope forward to the sand
With a greedy, silvered hand.

It is a horrible sound, the low wind's whistle
Across the seaweeds on the beach at night.
From stone to stone through hissing caves it passes
Up the curved cliff and shakes the prickly thistle
And spreads its hatred through the grasses.

In spite of that wicked sound
Of the wind that follows us like a scenting hound,
It is fitting on the curved cliff to remember the drowned,
To imagine them clearly for whom the sea no longer cares,
To deny the language of the thistle, to meet their foot-firm tread
Across the dark-sown tares
Who were skilful and erect, magnificent types of godhead,
To resist the dogging wind, to accuse the sea-god;
Yet in that gesture of anger we must admit
We were quarrelling with a phantom unawares.

For the sea turns whose every drop is counted
And the sand turns whose every grain a holy hour-glass holds
And the weeds turn beneath the sea, the sifted life slips free,

And the wave turns surrendering from its folds
All things that are not sea, and thrown off is the spirit
By the sea, the riderless horse which they once mounted.

Returning to Goleufryn

Returning to my grandfather's house, after this exile
From the coracle-river, long left with a coin to be good,
Returning with husks of those venturing ears for food
To lovely Carmarthen, I touch and remember the turnstile
Of this death-bound river. Fresh grass. Here I find that crown
In the shadow of dripping river-wood; then look up to the
    burning mile
Of windows. It is Goleufryn, the house on the hill;
And picking a child's path in a turn of the Towy I meet the
    prodigal town.

Sing, little house, clap hands: shut, like a book of the Psalms,
On the leaves and pressed flowers of a journey. All is sunny
In the garden behind you. The soil is alive with blind-petalled blooms
Plundered by bees. Gooseberries and currants are gay
With tranquil, unsettled light. Breathless light begging alms
Of the breathing grasses bent over the river of tombs
Flashes. A salmon has swallowed the tribute-money
Of the path. On the farther bank I see ragged urchins play

With thread and pin. O lead me that I may drown
In those earlier cobbles, reflected; a street that is strewn with palms,
Rustling with blouses and velvet. Yet I alone
By the light in the sunflower deepening, here stand, my eyes cast down
To the footprints of accusations, and hear the faint, leavening
Music of first Welsh words; that gust of plumes
'They shall mount up like eagles', dark-throated assumes,
Cold-sunned, low thunder and gentleness of the authentic Throne.

Yet now I am lost, lost in the water-wound looms
Where brief, square windows break on a garden's decay.
Gold butter is shining, the tablecloth speckled with crumbs.
The kettle throbs. In the calendar harvest is shown,

Standing in sheaves. Which way would I do you wrong?
Low, crumbling doorway of the infirm to the mansions of evening,
And poor, shrunken furrow where the potatoes are sown,
I shall not unnumber one soul I have stood with and known
To regain your stars struck by horses, your sons of God breaking in
      song.

The Feather

I stoop to gather a seabird's feather
Fallen on the beach,
Torn from a beautiful drifting wing;
What can I learn or teach,
Running my finger through the comb
And along the horny quill?
The body it was torn from
Gave out a cry so shrill,
Sailors looked from their white road
To see what help was there.
It dragged the winds to a drop of blood
Falling through drowned air,
Dropping from the sea-hawk's beak,
From frenzied talons sharp;
Now if the words they lost I speak
It must be to that harp
Under the strange, light-headed sea
That bears a straw of the nest.
Unless I make that melody,
How can the dead have rest?

Sheer from wide air to the wilderness
The victim fell, and lay;
The starlike bone is fathomless,
Lost among wind and spray.
This lonely, isolated thing
Trembles amid their sound.
I set my finger on the string
That spins the ages round.
But let it sleep, let it sleep

Where shell and stone are cast;
Its ecstasy the Furies keep,
For nothing here is past.
The perfect into night must fly;
On this the winds agree.
How could a blind rock satisfy
The hungers of the sea?

The Heron

The cloud-backed heron will not move:
He stares into the stream.
He stands unfaltering while the gulls
And oyster-catchers scream.
He does not hear, he cannot see
The great white horses of the sea,
But fixes eyes on stillness
Below their flying team.

How long will he remain, how long
Have the grey woods been green?
The sky and the reflected sky,
Their glass he has not seen,
But silent as a speck of sand
Interpreting the sea and land,
His fall pulls down the fabric
Of all that windy scene.

Sailing with clouds and woods behind,
Pausing in leisured flight,
He stepped, alighting on a stone,
Dropped from the stars of night.
He stood there unconcerned with day,
Deaf to the tumult of the bay,
Watching a stone in water,
A fish's hidden light.

Sharp rocks drive back the breaking waves,
Confusing sea with air.
Bundles of spray blown mountain-high
Have left the shingle bare.
A shipwrecked anchor wedged by rocks,
Loosed by the thundering equinox,
Divides the herded waters,
The stallion and his mare.

Yet no distraction breaks the watch
Of that time-killing bird.
He stands unmoving on the stone;
Since dawn he has not stirred.
Calamity about him cries,
But he has fixed his golden eyes
On water's crooked tablet,
On light's reflected word.

The Guest

All day, all night, wind and wild rain had blown;
Then the gale dropped, and in September weather
Where sunlight lingered on the pulse of stone
Red thistle and wild harebell shone together.

The cliff's crossed paths lay silvered with slug tracks
Where webs of hanging raindrops caught the sun.
A thrush with snail cocked sideways like an axe
Knocked with quick beak to crack it on a stone.

Stumbling, a blue-black beetle groped its way
Where crickets perched and dropped like jewelry.
Dawn's pestle mixed fresh colours for the day,
And, far beneath, a cormorant crossed the sea.

There was no guest to watch the landscape change.
All day slow, silken threads gold spiders spun.
Towards evening then I broke them, seeing a strange
Fleece in low heather catch the western sun.

There, halfway down the cliff, in fallen flight
I came on plumage, tufted claws, wide wings,
A white owl dead, feeding fritillary light
Into those roots from which the heather springs.

No wound appeared, though death had shrunk the eyes.
The bright wings held no marking but their own.
How close it lay no mouse dared recognise,
Lest it should pounce, and tear it to the bone.

A Prayer

If I dare pray for one
Gift in the coming age
That might protect my son
On every shifting stage
Keeping his joy as true
As now he feels in play
Fetching the ball I threw
Or pitched from day to day
Safe in a cot where sleep
Finds him still clasping toys
Until I step and stoop
And loose them with no noise,
I pray that he may have
Recourse in argument
After the falling wave
To what remains unspent,
That he may stoop and dare
To gather for his own
In that loud, hostile air
One word's deliberate throne,
I mean the uncounted praise,
The bridegroom's calm return
For which all nights and days
In speculation burn.
There where the breakers fly
Scattering their bridal lace,
Where instantly joy's eye

Rejects the commonplace,
Let him find strength to throw
Compromise to the winds
Though constancy forgo
All but his truest friends,
And patiently repair
The drift of broken vows,
Creating from despair
His Christ-appointed house,
That in the testing hour
Of hostile circumstance
His soul may put on power,
The impotence of chance
Revealing in his hold
On envy's taunting mind
Like Samson, tranquil-souled,
Who remained strong, though blind.

A Man with a Field

If I close my eyes I can see a man with a load of hay
Cross this garden, guiding his wheelbarrow through the copse
To a long, low green-house littered with earthenware, glass and clay,
Then prop his scythe near the sycamore to enter it, potted with seeds,
And pause where chrysanthemums grow, with tomatoes' dragonish
    beads.
Stooping to fasten the door, he turns on the path which leads
To his rain-pitted bedroom of 'cellos, and low jugs catching the
    drops.

If I open my eyes I see this musician-turned-ploughman slow,
Plainly follow his tractor vibrating beneath blue sky,
Or cast his sickle wide, or reach full-length with the hoe,
Or blame the weather that set its blight on a crop or a plan
To mend his roof, or cut back trees where convolvulus ran,
Or attend to as many needs as the holes in a watering-can:
He would wait for the better weather; it had been a wet July.

This year his field lay fallow; he was late putting down his seed.
Cold December concealed with a sighing surplice of snow
His waste of neglected furrows, overgrown with mutinous weed.
Dark, bereaved like the ground, I found him feeble and sick,
And cold, for neither the sticks nor his lamp with a shrunken wick
Would light. He was gone through the wicket. His clock continued to
    tick,
But it stopped when the new flakes clustered on an empty room
    below.

Waterfalls

Always in that valley in Wales I hear the noise
  Of waters falling.
              There is a clump of trees
  We climbed for nuts; and high in the trees the boys
    Lost in the rookery's cries
      Would cross, and branches cracking under their knees

Would break, and make in the winter wood new gaps.
  The leafmould covering the ground was almost black,
    But speckled and striped were the nuts we threw in our caps,
      Milked from split shells and cups,
        Secret as chestnuts when they are tipped from a sack,

Glossy and new.
           Always in that valley in Wales
  I hear that sound, those voices. They keep fresh
    What ripens, falls, drops into darkness, fails,
      Gone when dawn shines on scales,
        And glides from village memory, slips through the mesh,

And is not, when we come again.
          I look:
  Voices are under the bridge, and that voice calls,
    Now late, and answers;
          then, as the light twigs break
    Back, there is only the brook
      Reminding the stones where, under a breath, it falls.

Wordsworth

The barren mountains were his theme,
Nature the force that made him strong.
This day died one who, like a stone,
Altered the course of English song.

A hundred years! The waters still
Murmur the truth he bent to glean
Where bird and sunset, copse and hill
Composed the grave, harmonious scene.

The humble and unknown became
His oracles. Infirm old age
Matching obscurity to fame
Taught, like a child, the listening sage.

About his melancholy mind
Thundered the waterfalls. How few
Have left on water, light and wind
So calm a print of all he knew.

How cold the waters, yet how clear:
How grave the voice, how fine the thread
That quickening the returning year
Restores his landscape and his dead!

The Red Lady

They found red ochre in the cave
Of Paviland. The salt sea wave
Had left so many buried there,
But when one day the picks laid bare
Bones with the same red ochre dyed
It seemed they'd hit upon a bride
Whose burial rites had stained the mould.
Never was skeleton so old
In Britain found; but bones perplex
Their finders: they mistook her sex.

The rock deposits washed by springs
Had made those ancient colourings;
So the Red Lady's myth began
Before they found she was a man.
His bed the pollen's god waylaid,
But left a bed more safely made.
The moon's Red Lady sleeps the same,
True to her dark as when they came,
While he who took her image on
Now in the upper daylight shone,
Step by step, to be rebuilt
From antlered, prehistoric silt.
His coffin-bearers, halting, heard
The cry of many a wild seabird
Rise from a nest they could not hide.
Their shadows danced upon the tide
Protecting still, unknown to air,
The slender tissue in their care.

Strictness of Speech

Lord, defend us from the peroration.
Silence all that politicians say.
They who plough us in to make a nation
Have not known the vision we obey.

Wits that learn from mother-wit are keenest,
Nor is there nobility of style
Till the proud man kneels to help the meanest.
They who justify themselves are vile.

R. S. Thomas

Ronald Stuart Thomas is certainly the finest living Anglo-Welsh poet and his reputation has properly become international. He was born in Cardiff in 1913 and on leaving school attended University College, Bangor, where he gained a degree in Classics in 1935. He continued his studies at St Michael's College, Llandaff, and was ordained as a priest of the Church in Wales in 1937. His first parish was Manafon, Montgomeryshire, a remote, depopulated rural area, where he was Rector from 1942–54. On his own admission, he was shocked by the contrast between the comfortable, middle-class world which he had known and the comfortless, grinding toil of the hill-farmers of his parish. At first he was repelled:

> His clothes, sour with years of sweat
> And animal contact, shock the refined,
> But affected, sense . . .
>
> ('A Peasant')

but in the poems which he began to write out of his Manafon experience and which began to be published from about 1943, mainly in *Wales*, it was not long before repulsion turned to admiration of the stoic endurance of the peasant and awareness of his significance:

> Remember him, then, for he, too, is a winner of wars,
> Enduring like a tree.

The priest and the peasant share an isolation, the one unable to communicate adequately with his congregation:

> I am left alone
> With no echoes to the amen
> I dreamed of . . .
>
> ('Service')

the other 'so far in (his) small fields'.

44

R. S. Thomas's first volume of poetry, *The Stones of the Field*, was published by the Druid Press, Carmarthen, in 1946 and his second, *An Acre of Land*, by the Montgomeryshire Printing Co. in 1952. In 1954 he left Manafon for the similar, though less isolated, parish of Eglwysfach, Cardiganshire. In 1955, Hart-Davis published a collection of the poems written between 1942 and 1955, *Song at the Year's Turning*. The poet had by now established a reputation for his lucid, severe style and fine craftsmanship and as a questioning artist concerned not only with the individual peasants of rural Wales, but also with his own ministry among them and the history, culture and survival of his nation about which he tended to be pessimistic and bitter:

> an impotent people,
> Sick with inbreeding,
> Worrying the carcass of an old song.

('Welsh Landscape')

It has truly been said of him that his view of Wales is more like that of Gwenallt Jones and Saunders Lewis than that of, for example, Harri Webb, who, for all his concern, does see a *green* desert. From the time of *Poetry for Supper* (1958), volumes have appeared at more frequent intervals: *Tares* (1961), *The Bread of Truth* (1963), *Pietá* (1966), and the poet's established reputation has been recognised by such awards as the Heinemann Award of the Royal Society of Literature (1959), the Queen's Gold Medal for Poetry (1964) and Welsh Arts' Council prizes in 1967 and 1968. He has also written critically about poetry and he is in demand as a lecturer.

R. S. Thomas is now Rector of Aberdaron on the Llŷn peninsula of Caernarvonshire, responsible also for Rhiw and Llanfaelrhys where he takes the services in Welsh, a language which he has learned and in which he has wished to write poetry. Two further volumes have been published: *Not that He brought Flowers* (1968) and *H'm* (1972).

Unlike earlier priest/poets such as Gerard Manley Hopkins, R. S. Thomas finds no conflict between his vocations. In the documentary film made about him by John Ormond and broadcast in 1972 he said, 'poetry is religion, religion is poetry'. He is very committed – to the Word of God, to the nation, to the (often suffering) individual, the hill farmer 'stripped of love', Prytherch feeling the 'cold/Winds of the world blowing' after his encounter with the townee, Davies dying 'with his face to the wall'. Yet the picture is not always gloomy: 'Farm Child' and 'Cynddylan on a Tractor' show his perception of joy. The poet has chosen to spend his life in remote rural areas; he rejects modern industrial life (even Cynddylan's tractor is out of place), and compares the lonely moorland on which he likes to walk, significantly, to 'a quiet

45

church'. Yet he is never sentimental about Nature: he sees it as the work of God, but presents it most often as bleak and unforgiving.

The later poems are rather less melancholy than the early ones, but the poetry remains mainly sombre and the style sparing, of beautiful and striking clarity, controlled. R. S. Thomas, in contrast with Dylan Thomas, who wrote virtually all of his poetry when young and then declined, shows a steady, consistent progress. His subjects are, in one sense, narrow – Welsh landscape and history, religion, rural people, relationships – but they are given universal significance.

A Peasant

Iago Prytherch his name, though, be it allowed,
Just an ordinary man of the bald Welsh hills,
Who pens a few sheep in a gap of cloud.
Docking mangels, chipping the green skin
From the yellow bones with a half-witted grin
Of satisfaction, or churning the crude earth
To a stiff sea of clods that glint in the wind –
So are his days spent, his spittled mirth
Rarer than the sun that cracks the cheeks
Of the gaunt sky perhaps once in a week.
And then at night see him fixed in his chair
Motionless, except when he leans to gob in the fire.
There is something frightening in the vacancy of his mind.
His clothes, sour with years of sweat
And animal contact, shock the refined,
But affected, sense with their stark naturalness.
Yet this is your prototype, who, season by season
Against siege of rain and the wind's attrition,
Preserves his stock, an impregnable fortress
Not to be stormed even in death's confusion.
Remember him, then, for he, too, is a winner of wars,
Enduring like a tree under the curious stars.

Cynddylan on a Tractor

Ah, you should see Cynddylan on a tractor.
Gone the old look that yoked him to the soil;
He's a new man now, part of the machine,
His nerves of metal and his blood oil.
The clutch curses, but the gears obey
His least bidding, and lo, he's away
Out of the farmyard, scattering hens.
Riding to work now as a great man should,
He is the knight at arms breaking the fields'
Mirror of silence, emptying the wood
Of foxes and squirrels and bright jays.
The sun comes over the tall trees
Kindling all the hedges, but not for him
Who runs his engine on a different fuel.
And all the birds are singing, bills wide in vain,
As Cynddylan passes proudly up the lane.

The Hill Farmer Speaks

I am the farmer, stripped of love
And thought and grace by the land's hardness;
But what I am saying over the fields'
Desolate acres, rough with dew,
Is, Listen, listen, I am a man like you.

The wind goes over the hill pastures
Year after year, and the ewes starve,
Milkless, for want of the new grass.
And I starve, too, for something the spring
Can never foster in veins run dry.

The pig is a friend, the cattle's breath
Mingles with mine in the still lanes;
I wear it willingly like a cloak
To shelter me from your curious gaze.

The hens go in and out at the door
From sun to shadow, as stray thoughts pass
Over the floor of my wide skull.
The dirt is under my cracked nails;
The tale of my life is smirched with dung;
The phlegm rattles. But what I am saying
Over the grasses rough with dew
Is, Listen, listen, I am a man like you.

Invasion on the Farm

I am Prytherch. Forgive me. I don't know
What you are talking about; your thoughts flow
Too swiftly for me; I cannot dawdle
Along their banks and fish in their quick stream
With crude fingers. I am alone, exposed
In my own fields with no place to run
From your sharp eyes. I, who a moment back
Paddled in the bright grass, the old farm
Warm as a sack about me, feel the cold
Winds of the world blowing. The patched gate
You left open will never be shut again.

Death of a Peasant

You remember Davies? He died, you know,
With his face to the wall, as the manner is
Of the poor peasant in his stone croft
On the Welsh hills. I recall the room
Under the slates, and the smirched snow
Of the wide bed in which he lay,
Lonely as an ewe that is sick to lamb
In the hard weather of mid-March.
I remember also the trapped wind
Tearing the curtains, and the wild light's

Frequent hysteria upon the floor.
The bare floor without a rug
Or mat to soften the loud tread
Of neighbours crossing the uneasy boards
To peer at Davies with gruff words
Of meaningless comfort, before they turned
Heartless away from the stale smell
Of death in league with those dank walls.

Soil

A field with tall hedges and a young
Moon in the branches and one star
Declining westward set the scene
Where he works slowly astride the rows
Of red mangolds and green swedes
Plying mechanically his cold blade.

This is his world, the hedge defines
The mind's limits; only the sky
Is boundless, and he never looks up;
His gaze is deep in the dark soil,
As are his feet. The soil is all;
His hands fondle it, and his bones
Are formed out of it with the swedes.
And if sometimes the knife errs,
Burying itself in his shocked flesh,
Then out of the wound the blood seeps home
To the warm soil from which it came.

Welsh Landscape

To live in Wales is to be conscious
At dusk of the spilled blood
That went to the making of the wild sky,
Dyeing the immaculate rivers
In all their courses.
It is to be aware,
Above the noisy tractor
And hum of the machine
Of strife in the strung woods,
Vibrant with sped arrows.
You cannot live in the present,
At least not in Wales.
There is the language for instance,
The soft consonants
Strange to the ear.
There are cries in the dark at night
As owls answer the moon,
And thick ambush of shadows,
Hushed at the fields' corners
There is no present in Wales,
And no future;
There is only the past,
Brittle with relics,
Wind-bitten towers and castles
With sham ghosts;
Mouldering quarries and mines;
And an impotent people,
Sick with inbreeding,
Worrying the carcase of an old song.

Farm Child

Look at this village boy, his head is stuffed
With all the nests he knows, his pockets with flowers,
Snail-shells and bits of glass, the fruit of hours
Spent in the fields by thorn and thistle tuft.
Look at his eyes, see the harebell hiding there;

Mark how the sun has freckled his smooth face
Like a finch's egg under that bush of hair
That dares the wind, and in the mixen now
Notice his poise; from such unconscious grace
Earth breeds and beckons to the stubborn plough.

A Blackbird Singing

It seems wrong that out of this bird,
Black, bold, a suggestion of dark
Places about it, there yet should come
Such rich music, as though the notes'
Ore were changed to a rare metal
At one touch of that bright bill

You have heard it often, alone at your desk
In a green April, your mind drawn
Away from its work by sweet disturbance
Of the mild evening outside your room.

A slow singer, but loading each phrase
With history's overtones, love, joy
And grief learned by his dark tribe
In other orchards and passed on
Instinctively as they are now,
But fresh always with new tears.

Iago Prytherch

Iago Prytherch, forgive my naming you.
You are so far in your small fields
From the world's eye, sharpening your blade
On a cloud's edge, no one will tell you
How I made fun of you, or pitied either
Your long soliloquies, crouched at your slow
And patient surgery under the faint
November rays of the sun's lamp.

Made fun of you? That was their graceless
Accusation, because I took
Your rags for theme, because I showed them
Your thought's bareness; science and art,
The mind's furniture, having no chance
To install themselves, because of the great
Draught of nature sweeping the skull.

Fun? Pity? No word can describe
My true feelings. I passed and saw you
Labouring there, your dark figure
Marring the simple geometry
Of the square fields with its gaunt question.
My poems were made in its long shadow
Falling coldly across the page.

Lore

Job Davies, eighty-five
Winters old, and still alive
After the slow poison
And treachery of the seasons.

Miserable? Kick my arse!
It needs more than the rain's hearse,
Wind-drawn, to pull me off
The great perch of my laugh.

What's living but courage?
Paunch full of hot porridge,
Nerves strengthened with tea,
Peat-black, dawn found me

Mowing where the grass grew,
Bearded with golden dew.
Rhythm of the long scythe
Kept this tall frame lithe.

What to do? Stay green.
Never mind the machine,
Whose fuel is human souls.
Live large, man, and dream small.

Anniversary

Nineteen years now
Under the same roof
Eating our bread,
Using the same air;
Sighing, if one sighs,
Meeting the other's
Words with a look
That thaws suspicion.

Nineteen years now
Sharing life's table,
And not to be first
To call the meal long
We balance it thoughtfully
On the tip of the tongue,
Careful to maintain
The strict palate.

Nineteen years now
Keeping simple house,
Opening the door
To friend and stranger;

Opening the womb
Softly to let enter
The one child
With his huge hunger.

Ninetieth Birthday

You go up the long track
That will take a car, but is best walked
On slow foot, noting the lichen
That writes history on the page
Of the grey rock. Trees are about you
At first, but yield to the green bracken,
The nightjar's house: you can hear it spin
On warm evenings; it is still now
In the noonday heat, only the lesser
Voices sound, blue-fly and gnat
And the stream's whisper. As the road climbs,
You will pause for breath and the far sea's
Signal will flash, till you turn again
To the steep track, buttressed with cloud.

And there at the top that old woman,
Born almost a century back
In that stone farm, awaits your coming;
Waits for the news of the lost village
She thinks she knows, a place that exists
In her memory only.

You bring her greeting
And praise for having lasted so long
With time's knife shaving the bone.
Yet no bridge joins her own
World with yours, all you can do
Is lean kindly across the abyss
To hear words that were once wise.

Here

I am a man now.
Pass your hand over my brow,
You can feel the place where the brains grow.

I am like a tree,
From my top boughs I can see
The footprints that led up to me.

There is blood in my veins
That has run clear of the stain
Contracted in so many loins.

Why, then, are my hands red
With the blood of so many dead?
Is this where I was misled?

Why are my hands this way
That they will not do as I say?
Does not God hear when I pray?

I have nowhere to go.
The swift satellites show
The clock of my whole being is slow.

It is too late to start
For destinations not of the heart.
I must stay here with my hurt.

Sorry

Dear parents,
I forgive you my life,
Begotten in a drab town,
The intention was good;
Passing the street now,
I see still the remains of sunlight.

It was not the bone buckled;
You gave me enough food
To renew myself.
It was the mind's weight
Kept me bent, as I grew tall.

It was not your fault.
What should have gone on,
Arrow aimed from a tried bow
At a tried target, has turned back,
Wounding itself
With questions you had not asked.

For Instance

She gave me good food;
I accepted;

Sewed my clothes, buttons;
I was smart.

She warmed my bed;
Out of it my son stepped.

She was adjudged
Beautiful. I had grown

Used to it. She is dead
Now. Is it true

I loved her? That is how
I saw things. But not she.

A Welshman at St James' Park

I am invited to enter these gardens
As one of the public, and to conduct myself
In accordance with the regulations;
To keep off the grass and sample flowers
Without touching them; to admire birds
That have been seduced from wildness by
Bread they are pelted with.

                I am not one
Of the public; I have come a long way
To realise it. Under the sun's
Feathers are the sinews of stone,
The curved claws.

                I think of a Welsh hill
That is without fencing, and the men,
Bosworth blind, who left the heather
And the high pastures of the heart. I fumble
In the pocket's emptiness; my ticket
Was in two pieces. I kept half.

Service

We stand looking at
Each other. I take the word 'prayer'
And present it to them. I wait idly,
Wondering what their lips will
Make of it. But they hand back
Such presents. I am left alone
With no echoes to the amen
I dreamed of. I am saved by music
From the emptiness of this place
Of despair. As the melody rises
From nothing, their mouths take up the tune,
And the roof listens. I call on God
In the after silence, and my shadow
Wrestles with him upon a wall
Of plaster, that has all the nation's
Hardness in it. They see me thrown
Without movement of their oblique eyes.

No

And one said, This man can sing;
Let's listen to him. But the other,
Dirt on his mind, said, No, let's
Queer him. And the first, being weak,
Consented. So the Thing came
Nearer him, and its breath caused
Him to retch, and none knew why.
But he rested for one long month,
And after began to sing
For gladness, and the Thing stood,
Letting him, for a year, for two;
Then put out its raw hand
And touched him, and the wound took
Over, and the nurses wiped off
The poetry from his cracked lips.

Reservoirs

There are places in Wales I don't go:
Reservoirs that are the subconscious
Of a people, troubled far down
With gravestones, chapels, villages even;
The serenity of their expression
Revolts me, it is a pose
For strangers, a watercolour's appeal
To the mass, instead of the poem's
Harsher conditions. There are the hills,
Too; gardens gone under the scum
Of the forests; and the smashed faces
Of the farms with the stone trickle
Of their tears down the hills' side.

Where can I go, then, from the smell
Of decay, from the putrefying of a dead
Nation? I have walked the shore
For an hour and seen the English
Scavenging among the remains
Of our culture, covering the sand
Like the tide and, with the roughness
Of the tide, elbowing our language
Into the grave that we have dug for it.

Cain

Abel looked at the wound
His brother had dealt him, and loved him
For it. Cain saw that look
And struck him again. The blood cried
On the ground; God listened to it.
He questioned Cain. But Cain answered:
Who made the blood? I offered you
Clean things: the blond hair
Of the corn; the knuckled vegetables; the
Flowers; things that did not publish
Their hurt, that bled
Silently. You would not accept them.

And God said: It was part of myself
He gave me. The lamb was torn
From my own side. The limp head,
The slow fall of red tears – they
Were like a mirror to me in which I beheld
My reflection. I anointed myself
In readiness for the journey
To the doomed tree you were at work upon.

The Island

And God said, I will build a church here
And cause this people to worship me,
And afflict them with poverty and sickness
In return for centuries of hard work
And patience. And its walls shall be hard as
Their hearts, and its windows let in the light
Grudgingly, as their minds do, and the priest's words be drowned
By the wind's caterwauling. All this I will do,

Said God, and watch the bitterness in their eyes
Grow, and their lips suppurate with
Their prayers. And their women shall bring forth
On my altars, and I will choose the best
Of them to be thrown back into the sea.

And that was only on one island.

Dylan Thomas

Dylan Marlais Thomas was born in Swansea on 27 October 1914 of English-speaking, middle-class parents who had renounced their working-class, Welsh-speaking origins. Elocution lessons gave him a 'standard English' accent without spoiling the magnificent poetry-reading voice which we can still experience on the records that he made.

His father was senior English master at Swansea Grammar School, which he attended from 1925–31, publishing many poems, most of them comic, in the school magazine. Poems such as 'The Hunchback in the Park' show the importance of his Swansea upbringing, but he reacted against middle-class respectability in much the same spirit as the 'truant boys' of the poem. Rural West Wales was also important to him throughout his life, beginning with holidays spent in childhood with his aunt, Annie Jones, at Fern Hill Farm between Carmarthen and Llansteffan. Later he was to move to and be inspired by Laugharne, across the Tâf estuary from Llansteffan.

After leaving school he spent a year on the *South Wales Daily Post* – experience which must have helped him with stories, sketches, broadcasts and film-scripts later on. The years 1930–4 were astonishingly creative: during this period he wrote into his note-books an enormous quantity of poetry on which he was to draw virtually to the end of his life. 'And Death Shall Have No Dominion' was published in *The New English Weekly* in 1933, the year in which his correspondence with Pamela Hansford Johnson began. In 1934 he moved to London, supporting himself precariously with poems, stories and reviews. *Eighteen Poems*, his first volume, was published in 1934 and was a critical success. Apart from 'The Hand That Signed the Paper', however, he ignores the social and political issues that engaged other poets at that time.

Twenty-Five Poems was published in 1936, when he began to correspond with Vernon Watkins. In 1937 he married Caitlin Macnamara and in 1938 they spent some time in Laugharne. Llewelyn, the first of their three children, was born in 1939 and during the Second World War, having been found unfit for the Army, Thomas joined the B.B.C. He made many broadcasts and wrote radio and film-scripts. His poetry was influenced by the war as can be seen from 'A Refusal to Mourn'.

After the war his broadcasts continued: he made more than 80 between 1945 and 1947. Between 1945 and 1949 he was living in London and Oxford, with visits to Ireland, Italy and Prague. *Deaths and Entrances*, his third volume, was published in 1946. He was constantly in financial difficulties and from 1950 onwards made four reading and lecturing tours to the U.S.A., living, when in England, at Laugharne. Only at the very end of his life did he begin to make money from his poetry, though from the first his originality and genius had been recognised. In 1952 his fourth volume, *In Country Sleep* was published; the *Collected Poems* which came out in the same year won Foyle's Poetry Prize and was to sell 30,000 copies, but too late to help him. He died in New York on 9 November 1953, the famous 'play for voices', *Under Milk Wood*, being published posthumously in 1954 after an immense broadcasting success.

He should not be judged on this final work, for though a striking success it is not in the same class as the poetry. The latter, at its best, is powerful, keenly intelligent, often astonishingly skilled and elaborate in form and difficult, mainly because of its surrealist qualities (he was associated with the poetic movement known as 'The New Apocalypse') in content:

> Where once the mermen through your ice
> Pushed up their hair, the dry wind steers.

An intense awareness of sexual passion and of death come together in fine poems such as 'And Death Shall Have No Dominion':

> Though lovers be lost love shall not;
> And death shall have no dominion.

He followed no orthodox faith, but traditional religious imagery is of fundamental importance to his work (see 'This Bread I Break') and is commonly linked with imagery from nature ('A Refusal'):

> I must enter again the round
> Zion of the water bead
> And the synagogue of the ear of corn.

His use of words is musical, lyrical, excited and exciting. Some of the finest poetry deals with the intensity of experience associated with childhood and adolescence:

Where a boy
In the listening
Summertime of the dead whispered the truth of his joy
To the trees and the stones and the fish in the tide.

Here, very much like the Wordsworth of 'Tintern Abbey', he looks back with a feeling of inspiration lost. The apparent spontaneity of work such as this is, it must be realised, the product of a most intense and painstaking craftsmanship.

I Have Longed to Move Away

I have longed to move away
From the hissing of the spent lie
And the old terrors' continual cry
Growing more terrible as the day
Goes over the hill into the deep sea;
I have longed to move away
From the repetition of salutes,
From there are ghosts in the air
And ghostly echoes on paper,
And the thunder of calls and notes.

I have longed to move away but am afraid;
Some life, yet unspent, might explode
Out of the old lie burning on the ground,
And, crackling into the air, leave me half-blind.
Neither by night's ancient fear,
The parting of hat from hair,
Pursed lips at the receiver,
Shall I fall to death's feather.
By these I would not care to die,
Half convention and half lie.

And Death Shall Have No Dominion

And death shall have no dominion.
Dead men naked they shall be one
With the man in the wind and the west moon;
When their bones are picked clean and the clean bones gone,
They shall have stars at elbow and foot;
Though they go mad they shall be sane,
Though they sink through the sea they shall rise again;
Though lovers be lost love shall not
And death shall have no dominion.

And death shall have no dominion.
Under the windings of the sea
They lying long shall not die windily;
Twisting on racks when sinews give way,
Strapped to a wheel, yet they shall not break;
Faith in their hands shall snap in two,
And the unicorn evils run them through;
Split all ends up they shan't crack;
And death shall have no dominion.

And death shall have no dominion.
No more may gulls cry at their ears
Or waves break loud on the seashores;
Where blew a flower may a flower no more
Lift its head to the blows of the rain;
Though they be mad and dead as nails,
Heads of the characters hammer through daisies;
Break in the sun till the sun breaks down,
And death shall have no dominion.

The Hand That Signed the Paper

The hand that signed the paper felled a city;
Five sovereign fingers taxed the breath,
Doubled the globe of dead and halved a country;
These five kings did a king to death.

The mighty hand leads to a sloping shoulder,
The finger joints are cramped with chalk;
A goose's quill has put an end to murder
That put an end to talk.

The hand that signed the treaty bred a fever,
And famine grew, and locusts came;
Great is the hand that holds dominion over
Man by a scribbled name.

The five kings count the dead but do not soften
The crusted wound nor stroke the brow;
A hand rules pity as a hand rules heaven;
Hands have no tears to flow.

Light Breaks Where No Sun Shines

Light breaks where no sun shines;
Where no sea runs, the waters of the heart
Push in their tides;
And, broken ghosts with glow-worms in their heads,
The things of light
File through the flesh where no flesh decks the bones.

A candle in the thighs
Warms youth and seed and burns the seeds of age;
Where no seed stirs,
The fruit of man unwrinkles in the stars,
Bright as a fig;
Where no wax is, the candle shows its hairs.

Dawn breaks behind the eyes;
From poles of skull and toe the windy blood
Slides like a sea;
Nor fenced, nor staked, the gushers of the sky
Spout to the rod
Divining in a smile the oil of tears.

Night in the sockets rounds,
Like some pitch moon, the limit of the globes;
Day lights the bone;
Where no cold is, the skinning gales unpin
The winter's robes;
The film of spring is hanging from the lids.

Light breaks on secret lots,
On tips of thought where thoughts smell in the rain;
When logics die,
The secret of the soil grows through the eye,
And blood jumps in the sun;
Above the waste allotments the dawn halts.

This Bread I Break

This bread I break was once the oat,
This wine upon a foreign tree
Plunged in its fruit;
Man in the day or wind at night
Laid the crops low, broke the grape's joy.

Once in this wine the summer blood
Knocked in the flesh that decked the vine,
Once in this bread
The oat was merry in the wind;
Man broke the sun, pulled the wind down.

This flesh you break, this blood you let
Make desolation in the vein,
Were oat and grape
Born of the sensual root and sap;
My wine you drink, my bread you snap.

Where Once the Waters of Your Face

Where once the waters of your face
Spun to my screws, your dry ghost blows,
The dead turns up its eye;
Where once the mermen through your ice
Pushed up their hair, the dry wind steers
Through salt and root and roe.

Where once your green knots sank their splice
Into the tided cord, there goes
The green unraveller,
His scissors oiled, his knife hung loose
To cut the channels at their source
And lay the wet fruits low.

Invisible, your clocking tides
Break on the lovebeds of the weeds;
The weed of love's left dry;
There round about your stones the shades
Of children go who, from their voids,
Cry to the dolphined sea.

Dry as a tomb, your coloured lids
Shall not be latched while magic glides
Sage on the earth and sky;
There shall be corals in your beds,
There shall be serpents in your tides,
Till all our sea-faiths die.

Once It Was the Colour of Saying

Once it was the colour of saying
Soaked my table the uglier side of a hill
With a capsized field where a school sat still
And a black and white patch of girls grew playing;
The gentle seaslides of saying I must undo
That all the charmingly drowned arise to cockcrow and kill.
When I whistled with mitching boys through a reservoir park

Where at night we stoned the cold and cuckoo
Lovers in the dirt of their leafy beds,
The shade of their trees was a word of many shades
And a lamp of lightning for the poor in the dark;
Now my saying shall be my undoing,
And every stone I wind off like a reel.

The Hunchback in the Park

The hunchback in the park
A solitary mister
Propped between trees and water
From the opening of the garden lock
That lets the trees and water enter
Until the Sunday sombre bell at dark

Eating bread from a newspaper
Drinking water from the chained cup
That the children filled with gravel
In the fountain basin where I sailed my ship
Slept at night in a dog kennel
But nobody chained him up.

Like the park birds he came early
Like the water he sat down
And Mister they called Hey mister
The truant boys from the town
Running when he had heard them clearly
On out of sound

Past lake and rockery
Laughing when he shook his paper
Hunchbacked in mockery
Through the loud zoo of the willow groves
Dodging the park keeper
With his stick that picked up leaves.

And the old dog sleeper
Alone between nurses and swans
While the boys among willows
Made the tigers jump out of their eyes
To roar on the rockery stones
And the groves were blue with sailors

Made all day until bell time
A woman figure without fault
Straight as a young elm
Straight and tall from his crooked bones
That she might stand in the night
After the locks and chains

All night in the unmade park
After the railings and shrubberies
The birds the grass the trees the lake
And the wild boys innocent as strawberries
Had followed the hunchback
To his kennel in the dark.

Poem in October

It was my thirtieth year to heaven
Woke to my hearing from harbour and neighbour wood
And the mussel pooled and the heron
Priested shore
The morning beckon
With water praying and call of seagull and rook
And the knock of sailing boats on the net webbed wall
Myself to set foot
That second
In the still sleeping town and set forth.

My birthday began with the water –
Birds and the birds of the winged trees flying my name
Above the farms and the white horses
And I rose
In the rainy autumn

And walked abroad in a shower of all my days.
High tide and the heron dived when I took the road
   Over the border
   And the gates
Of the town closed as the town awoke.

  A springful of larks in a rolling
Cloud and the roadside bushes brimming with whistling
   Blackbirds and the sun of October
    Summery
    On the hill's shoulder,
Here were fond climates and sweet singers suddenly
Come in the morning where I wandered and listened
   To the rain wringing
   Wind blow cold
In the wood faraway under me.

  Pale rain over the dwindling harbour
And over the sea wet church the size of a snail
   With its horns through mist and the castle
    Brown as owls
    But all the gardens
Of spring and summer were blooming in the tall tales
Beyond the border and under the lark full cloud
   There could I marvel
   My birthday
Away but the weather turned around.

  It turned away from the blithe country
And down the other air and the blue altered sky
   Streamed again a wonder of summer
    With apples
    Pears and red currants
And I saw in the turning so clearly a child's
Forgotten mornings when he walked with his mother
   Through the parables
   Of sun light
And the legends of the green chapels

  And the twice told fields of infancy
That his tears burned my cheeks and his heart moved in mine.
   These were the woods the river and sea

Where a boy
In the listening
Summertime of the dead whispered the truth of his joy
To the trees and the stones and the fish in the tide.
And the mystery
Sang alive
Still in the water and singingbirds.

And there could I marvel my birthday
Away but the weather turned around. And the true
Joy of the long dead child sang burning
In the sun.
It was my thirtieth
Year to heaven stood there then in the summer noon
Though the town below lay leaved with October blood.
O may my heart's truth
Still be sung
On this high hill in a year's turning.

A Refusal to Mourn the Death, by Fire, of a Child in London

Never until the mankind making
Bird beast and flower
Fathering and all humbling darkness
Tells with silence the last light breaking
And the still hour
Is come of the sea tumbling in harness

And I must enter again the round
Zion of the water bead
And the synagogue of the ear of corn
Shall I let pray the shadow of a sound
Or sow my salt seed
In the least valley of sackcloth to mourn

The majesty and burning of the child's death.
I shall not murder
The mankind of her going with a grave truth
Nor blaspheme down the stations of the breath
With any further
Elegy of innocence and youth.

Deep with the first dead lies London's daughter,
Robed in the long friends,
The grains beyond age, the dark veins of her mother,
Secret by the unmourning water
Of the riding Thames.
After the first death, there is no other.

In My Craft or Sullen Art

In my craft or sullen art
Exercised in the still night
When only the moon rages
And the lovers lie abed
With all their griefs in their arms,
I labour by singing light
Not for ambition or bread
Or the strut and trade of charms
On the ivory stages
But for the common wages
Of their most secret heart.

Not for the proud man apart
From the raging moon I write
On these spindrift pages
Nor for the towering dead
With their nightingales and psalms
But for the lovers, their arms
Round the griefs of the ages,
Who pay no praise or wages
Nor heed my craft or art.

Alun Lewis

A Glamorganshire man, born on 1 July 1915 at Cwmaman, a small mining village near Aberdare. His father was a teacher who later became Director of Education for Aberdare; his mother was the daughter of a Welsh Unitarian minister. He was the eldest of a family of four, having two brothers and a sister. He attended Cowbridge Grammar School as a boarder from 1926 and while there published short stories in the school magazine. He gained First Class Honours in History at Aberystwyth in 1935, led a full social life and published short stories and a poem in *The Dragon*. He spent two years doing research into medieval history at Manchester, published more short stories in the Owen's College magazine and attended an international peace conference in North France in 1937. He took the Post-Graduate Certificate in Education at Aberystwyth in 1938 and at about this time began to get poems published in *The Observer* and *Time and Tide*.

Unable to obtain a teaching post at first, he worked for a time as a journalist on *The Aberdare Leader* until he joined the staff of Pengam School in November 1938. He was an effective and popular teacher. In 1939 he became engaged to Gweno Ellis whom he married in 1941. He enlisted in the Army in spring 1940 and one of his short stories won the O'Brien Short Story Award in 1941. In the same year he was associated with Brenda Chamberlain and John Petts in the *Caseg Broadsheets*, an attempt to bring Welsh poetry to ordinary people. He became an officer.

In 1942 *Raiders' Dawn*, his first collection of poems, was published by Allen and Unwin and sold well. In the same year the same publisher brought out *The Last Inspection and Other Stories*, most of which are concerned with Army life.

In November 1942 his regiment was posted to India where they were prepared for fighting against the Japanese. Six weeks in hospital in 1943 produced poems such as 'In Hospital: Poona' and during his brief time in India he wrote a great many poems. He turned down the

73

chance of a comparatively safe and easy life as a staff officer out of loyalty to his men. In 1944 his regiment was moved to Burma where, on 5 March, he died as the result of a revolver accident. His second (and last) book of poems, selected by him shortly before his death, was *Ha! Ha! Among the Trumpets*, published posthumously in 1945.

As a man he was inclined to be shy at first meeting, but, though serious, he was sociable and had a great sense of fun. He genuinely liked people and, as his poetry shows, sympathised deeply with them. He was highly intelligent, but also a vigorous sportsman, particularly at hockey and boxing. From his childhood he had a love for nature, especially the mountains and the sea, and the sense of landscape is prominent in the poetry. Though always a humble man, he was honest and forthright in the expression of his deep convictions.

He wrote short stories before he wrote poetry and is a notable writer in this field – at one stage he considered writing a novel. In all his work there is a concern for suffering humanity, whether it be the men with whom he served

> Sharing Life's iron rations, marching light,
> Enduring to the end the early cold,
> The emptiness of noon, the void of night . . .

('Infantry')

the people of the Welsh mining valleys, or the peasants of India

> The women breaking stones upon the highway,
> Walking erect with burdens on their heads.

('The Peasants')

In this he is comparable with the First World War poet, Edward Thomas, whom he admired. He was the first and is arguably the best of the poets of the Second World War. His poetry is sensitive, often sad:

> I watch the clouded years
> Rune the rough foreheads of these moody hills,
> This wet evening, in a lost age.

('The Mountain Over Aberdare')

It has a musical and lyrical quality that comes over most clearly when he is expressing his profound love for his wife:

> We made the universe to be our home,
> Our nostrils took the wind to be our breath,
> Our hearts are massive towers of delight,
> We stride across the seven seas of death.

('Goodbye')

74

Always aware of the hard struggle of life, he expresses it with truth, gentleness and humility.

Raiders' Dawn

Softly the civilised
Centuries fall,
Paper on paper,
Peter on Paul.

And lovers waking
From the night –
Eternity's masters,
Slaves of Time –
Recognise only
The drifting white
Fall of small faces
In pits of lime.

Blue necklace left
On a charred chair
Tells that Beauty
Was startled there.

The Rhondda

Hum of shaft-wheel, whirr and clamour
Of steel hammers overbeat, din down
Water-hag's slander. Greasy Rhondda
River throws about the boulders
Veils of scum to mark the ancient
Degraded union of stone and water.

Unwashed colliers by the river
Gamble for luck the pavements hide.

Kids float tins down dirty rapids.
Coal-dust rings the scruffy willows.
Circe is a drab.
She gives men what they know.
Daily to her pitch-black shaft
Her whirring wheels suck husbands out of sleep.
She for her profit takes their hands and eyes.

But the fat flabby-breasted wives
Have grown accustomed to her ways.
They scrub, make tea, peel the potatoes
Without counting the days.

The Mountain Over Aberdare

From this high quarried ledge I see
The place for which the Quakers once
Collected clothes, my fathers' home,
Our stubborn bankrupt village sprawled
In jaded dusk beneath its nameless hills;
The drab streets strung across the cwm,
Derelict workings, tips of slag
The gospellers and gamblers use
And children scrutting for the coal
That winter dole cannot purvey;
Allotments where the collier digs
While engines hack the coal within his brain;
Grey Hebron in a rigid cramp,
White cheap-jack cinema, the church
Stretched like a sow beside the stream;
And mourners in their Sunday best
Holding a tiny funeral, singing hymns
That drift insidious as the rain
Which rises from the steaming fields
And swathes about the skyline crags
Till all the upland gorse is drenched
And all the creaking mountain gates
Drip brittle tears of crystal peace;
And in a curtained parlour women hug
Huge grief, and anger against God.

But now the dusk, more charitable than Quakers,
Veils the cracked cottages with drifting may
And rubs the hard day off the slate.
The colliers squatting on the ashtip
Listen to one who holds them still with tales,
While that white frock that floats down the dark alley
Looks just like Christ; and in the lane
The clink of coins among the gamblers
Suggests the thirty pieces of silver.

I watch the clouded years
Rune the rough foreheads of these moody hills,
This wet evening, in a lost age.

The Defeated

'Sooner will his blood be spent than he go to the wedding feast.
No hatred shall there be between thee and me; better will I do to
thee, to praise thee in song.'   (A Welsh poem: 7th–9th century)

Our courage is an old legend.
We left the fields of our fathers.
Fate was our foeman.

We held the world in our fingers
And threw it like a farthing
That needed no keeping.

More love was there never
By Euphrates and Tigris
Than in our proud country.

Love was our talisman.
We were blinded in battle
By the weeping of women.

Bled white are our wounds,
Wounds writhing with worms;
All spilt the quick seed . . .

Oh! dark are we whose greed for life
Was a green slash in our eyes
And in our darkness we are wise,

Forgetting honour, valour, fame,
In this darkness whence we came.

All Day It Has Rained

All day it has rained, and we on the edge of the moors
Have sprawled in our bell-tents, moody and dull as boors,
Groundsheets and blankets spread on the muddy ground
And from the first grey wakening we have found
No refuge from the skirmishing fine rain
And the wind that made the canvas heave and flap
And the taut wet guy-ropes ravel out and snap.
All day the rain has glided, wave and mist and dream,
Drenching the gorse and heather, a gossamer stream
Too light to stir the acorns that suddenly
Snatched from their cups by the wild south-westerly
Pattered against the tent and our upturned dreaming faces.
And we stretched out, unbuttoning our braces,
Smoking a Woodbine, darning dirty socks,
Reading the Sunday papers – I saw a fox
And mentioned it in the note I scribbled home; –
And we talked of girls, and dropping bombs on Rome,
And thought of the quiet dead and the loud celebrities
Exhorting us to slaughter, and the herded refugees;
– Yet thought softly, morosely of them, and as indifferently
As of ourselves or those whom we
For years have loved, and will again
Tomorrow maybe love; but now it is the rain
Possesses us entirely, the twilight and the rain.

And I can remember nothing dearer or more to my heart
Than the children I watched in the woods on Saturday
Shaking down burning chestnuts for the schoolyard's merry play,

Or the shaggy patient dog who followed me
By Sheet and Steep and up the wooded scree
To the Shoulder o' Mutton where Edward Thomas brooded long
On death and beauty – till a bullet stopped his song.

Infantry

By day these men ask nothing, and obey;
They eat their bread behind a heap of stones;
Hardship and violence grow an easy way,
Winter is like a girl within their bones.

They learn the gambits of the soul,
Think lightly of the themes of life and death,
All mortal anguish shrunk into an ache
Too nagging to be worth the catch of breath.

Sharing Life's iron rations, marching light,
Enduring to the end the early cold,
The emptiness of noon, the void of night
In whose black market they are bought and sold;
They take their silent stations for the fight.
Rum's holy unction makes the dubious bold.

A Welsh Night

Fine flame of silver birches flickers
Along the coal-tipped misty slopes
Of old Garth mountain who tonight
Lies grey as a sermon of patience
For the threadbare congregations of the anxious.
Huddled in black-out rows the streets
Hoard the hand-pressed human warmth
Of families round a soap-scrubbed table;

Munition girls with yellow hands
Clicking bone needles over khaki scarves,
Schoolboys' painful numerals in a book,
A mother's chilblained fingers soft
Upon the bald head of a suckling child,
But no man in the house to clean the grate
Or bolt the outside door or share the night.
Yet everywhere through cracks of light
Faint strokes of thoughtfulness feel out
Into the throbbing night's malevolence,
And turn its hurt to gentler ways.

Hearing the clock strike midnight by the river
This village buried deeper than the corn
Bows its blind head beneath the angelic planes,
And cherishing all known and suffered harm
It wears the darkness like a shroud or shawl.

The Peasants

The dwarf barefooted, chanting
Behind the oxen by the lake,
Stepping lightly and lazily among the thorn trees
Dusky and dazed with sunlight, half-awake;

The women breaking stones upon the highway,
Walking erect with burdens on their heads,
One body growing in another body,
Creation touching verminous straw beds.

Across scorched hills and trampled crops
The soldiers straggle by.
History staggers in their wake.
The peasants watch them die.

Bivouac

There was no trace of Heaven
That night as we lay
Punch-drunk and blistered with sunlight
On the ploughed-up clay.

I remembered the cactus where our wheels
Had bruised it, bleeding white;
And a fat rat crouching beadyeyed
Caught by my light;

And the dry disturbing whispers
Of the agitated wood,
With its leathery vendetta,
Mantillas dark with blood.

And the darkness drenched with Evil
Haunting as a country song,
Ignoring the protesting cry
Of Right and of Wrong.

Yet the peasant was drawing water
With the first excited bird
And the dawn with childish eyes
Observed us as we stirred

And the milk-white oxen waited
Docile at the yoke
As we clipped on our equipment
And scarcely spoke

Being bewildered by the night
And only aware
Of the withering obsession
That lovers grow to fear
When the last note is written
And at last and alone
One of them wakes in terror
And the other is gone.

The Crucifixion

From the first he would not avoid it.
He knew they would stone and defile him, and looked to it calmly,
Riding to meet it serenely across the palm leaves, –
Processions in the East being near to bloodshed, –
Foreseeing a time when the body and all its injunctions
And *life* and *people* and all their persistent demands
Would desist, and they'd leave a policeman
Outside his door or his tomb to keep all in order
While he lay in supremest consummate passion
Passively passionate, suffering suffering only.

And this surrender of self to a greater statement
Has been desired by many more humble than he.
But when it came, was it other than he had imagined?
Breaking his Self up, convulsing his Father in pain?
His will prevented by every throbbing stigma,
The pangs that puffed and strained his stomach wall,
The utter weariness that bowed his head,
Taught him perhaps that more hung on the presence
Of all the natural preoccupations,
Duties, emotions, daily obligations
Affections and responses than he'd guessed.
They'd grown a burden to him, but as a mother
Is burdened by her child's head when her breasts
Are thin and milkless; he knew this awful hanging
Obscene with urine, sagging on a limb,
Was not the End of life, and improved nothing.

The Mahratta Ghats

The valleys crack and burn, the exhausted plains
Sink their black teeth into the horny veins
Straggling the hills' red thighs, the bleating goats
– Dry bents and bitter thistles in their throats –
Thread the loose rocks by immemorial tracks.
Dark peasants drag the sun upon their backs.

High on the ghat the new turned soil is red,
The sun has ground it to the finest red,
It lies like gold within each horny hand.
Siva has spilt his seed upon this land.

Will she who burns and withers on the plain
Leave, ere too late, her scraggy herds of pain,
The cow-dung fire and the trembling beasts,
The little wicked gods, the grinning priests,
And climb, before a thousand years have fled,
High as the eagle to her mountain bed
Whose soil is fine as flour and blood-red?

But no! She cannot move. Each arid patch
Owns the lean folk who plough and scythe and thatch
Its grudging yield and scratch its stubborn stones.
The small gods suck the marrow from their bones.

Who is it climbs the summit of the road?
Only the beggar bumming his dark load.
Who was it cried to see the falling star?
Only the landless soldier lost in war.

And did a thousand years go by in vain?
And does another thousand start again?

In Hospital: Poona (1)

Last night I did not fight for sleep
But lay awake from midnight while the world
Turned its slow features to the moving deep
Of darkness, till I knew that you were furled,

Beloved, in the same dark watch as I.
And sixty degrees of longitude beside
Vanished as though a swan in ecstasy
Had spanned the distance from your sleeping side.

And like to swan or moon the whole of Wales
Glided within the parish of my care:
I saw the green tide leap on Cardigan,
Your red yacht riding like a legend there,

And the great mountains, Dafydd and Llewelyn,
Plynlimmon, Cader Idris and Eryri
Threshing the darkness back from head and fin,
And also the small nameless mining valley

Whose slopes are scratched with streets and sprawling graves
Dark in the lap of firwoods and great boulders
Where you lay waiting, listening to the waves –
My hot hands touched your white despondent shoulders

– And then ten thousand miles of daylight grew
Between us, and I heard the wild daws crake
In India's starving throat; whereat I knew
That Time upon the heart can break
But love survives the venom of the snake.

Song

I lay in sheets of softest linen
Sleepless and my lover spoke
The word of Death within her sleep
And snuggled closer and awoke
And wrapped me in her snowwhite cloak,

And clasped me in exhausted arms
And swore I should not go again.
Her lips were writhing like a moth
Burnt in the steady lamp of pain.
But I was young and fain.

I heard the daylight wind its horn,
I saw the cloudy horsemen ride.
But my beloved lacked the strength
To keep me by her side
And I went forth in pride.

I clasped the burning sun all day,
The cold moon bled me white;
Then all things ended suddenly.
I saw the world take flight
And glitter in the starry night.

Goodbye

So we must say Goodbye, my darling,
And go, as lovers go, for ever;
Tonight remains, to pack and fix on labels
And make an end of lying down together.

I put a final shilling in the gas,
And watch you slip your dress below your knees
And lie so still I hear your rustling comb
Modulate the autumn in the trees.

And all the countless things I shall remember
Lay mummy-cloths of silence round my head;
I fill the carafe with a drink of water;
You say 'We paid a guinea for this bed,'

And then, 'We'll leave some gas, a little warmth
For the next resident, and these dry flowers,'
And turn your face away, afraid to speak
The big word, that Eternity is ours.

Your kisses close my eyes and yet you stare
As though God struck a child with nameless fears;
Perhaps the water glitters and discloses
Time's chalice and its limpid useless tears.

Everything we renounce except our selves;
Selfishness is the last of all to go;
Our sighs are exhalations of the earth,
Our footprints leave a track across the snow.

We made the universe to be our home,
Our nostrils took the wind to be our breath,
Our hearts are massive towers of delight,
We stride across the seven seas of death.

Yet when all's done you'll keep the emerald
I placed upon your finger in the street;
And I will keep the patches that you sewed
On my old battledress tonight, my sweet.

Roland Mathias

Roland Glyn Mathias was born at Talybont-on-Usk, Breconshire, on 4 September 1915 and although he has lived and worked far from his home area (since his retirement he has returned to it), it has been very important to his inspiration:

> Listen, Caerfanell, who gave me a fish for my stone,
> Listen, I am alone, alone.
> And Grwyney, both your rivers are one in the end
> And are loved.
>
> ('The Flooded Valley')

He was educated at Caterham School and Jesus College, Oxford, where he gained a First Class Honours degree in Modern History in 1936. The historical bent of his mind is evident in the poetry, not only in a fondness for writing of past events and earlier experiences in an attempt to discover their, and his own, significance, but also in the sense (which he shares with other Anglo-Welsh poets, notably R. S. Thomas) of the historical associations of a landscape:

> They ghosted every shift, farming
> A memory of that last-seen
> Country that was never theirs.
>
> ('They Have Not Survived')

He took a B.Litt. in 1939 and an M.A. in 1944. He married Mary (Molly) Howes, and they have a son and two daughters.

He has now retired to devote himself entirely to writing and to the editorship of *The Anglo-Welsh Review*, but he has had a distinguished career as teacher and headmaster: Pembroke Dock Grammar School from 1948–58 (when he was associated with Raymond Garlick in the founding of *Dock Leaves* which became *The Anglo-Welsh Review*); the Herbert Strutt School, Belper, Derbyshire (1958–64) and King Edward's Five Ways School, Birmingham (1964–9).

87

His first published poetry was the volume *Days Enduring* (Stockwell, Ilfracombe, 1943). In 1946, Routledge published *Break in Harvest*, and *The Roses of Tretower* was printed by the Dock Leaves Press in 1952. In 1960, *The Flooded Valley* was published by Putnam; he won a Welsh Arts' Council Writers' Award in 1969 and his latest volume is *Absalom in the Tree* (Gwasg Gomer, Llandysul, 1971). He has also written a large number of short stories and done a great deal of significant critical work.

Three aspects of his work are likely to strike the reader at once: its difficulty, its concern with place, its memorable and compassionate portrayal of individual characters. The difficulty is most noticeable in the early poems and is often the result of his very distinctive style:

> Each lamb unshrives
> His fellow and fine the day is with a laverock shimmer.
>
> ('Hawk')

Here the unusual 'unshrives' and 'laverock shimmer' are striking and compel the reader to pause for thought which results in his seeing the picture the more clearly. In 'For Warren Davies', however, we find:

> And jawed like Magnus at the holocaust.
> A crab for history, . . .

which appears to be wilfully obscure and to impede rather than to deepen one's appreciation. Of the importance of place the poet himself has said: 'In my earlier poetry the sense of "place" was very strong . . . Even love poems used the "place" or "history" symbol.' He can involve us deeply in a memorable scene either urban, as in 'Argyle Street', or rural ('Craswall'), though his purpose is rarely mere description. 'Freshwater West', for example, uses the beautifully evoked movement of waves to lead, almost hypnotically, into an elucidation of feelings:

> Beat till the few and best of these summers
> Of mine are as sand, over
> And many and meaningless . . .

The latter poems grow more concerned with people ('For An Unmarked Grave'; 'They Have Not Survived'; 'A Letter From Gwyther Street'). The best of them is 'For Warren Davies', of which the opening lines typify the poet's ability to make us *see* his subject:

> How best remember? Shipwright you, quiet, wry
> As a hawk, a viking-cast dropped out of conquest,

and demonstrate again the power of his distinctive style.

Throughout the poetry, especially the later poetry, runs a deep sense of melancholy, regret for earlier days:

Not a mark of my passing anywhere, only
Sea eating the whiter sift . . .

There is also controlled anger about the exploitation of Wales which has driven farmers from their land ('The Flooded Valley') exhausted miners and then cast them aside ('They Have Not Survived') – and it is, realistically, coupled with self-criticism: 'Why am I unlike/Them, alive and jack in office'.

The Flooded Valley

My house is empty but for a pair of boots:
The reservoir slaps at the privet hedge and uncovers the roots
And afterwards pats them up with a slack good will:
The sheep that I market once are not again to sell.
I am no waterman, and who of the others will live
Here, feeling the ripple spreading, hearing the timbers grieve?
The house I was born in has not long to stand:
My pounds are slipping away and will not wait for the end.

I will pick up my boots and run round the shire
To raise an echo louder than my fear.
Listen, Caerfanell, who gave me a fish for my stone,
Listen, I am alone, alone.
And Grwyney, both your rivers are one in the end
And are loved. If I command
You to remember me, will you, will you,
Because I was once at noon by your painted church of Patricio?
You did not despise me once, Senni, or run so fast
From your lovers. And O I jumped over your waist
Before sunrise or the flower was warm on the gorse.
You would do well to listen, Senni. There is money in my purse.

So you are quiet, all of you, and your current set away
Cautiously from the chapel ground in which my people lie . . .
Am I not Kedward, Prosser, Morgan, whose long stones
Name me despairingly and set me chains?

If I must quarrel and scuff in the weeds of another shire
When my pounds are gone, swear to me now in my weakness, swear
To me poor you will plant a stone more in this tightening field
And name there your latest dead, alas your unweaned feeblest child.

Hawk

There are marks of snow on the goitred neck
Where the cut begins. Grey clouds concentrate
In a mountain hurly-burly shoulder
To shoulder. Buffet and Jehu-crack
Predominate. Slowly the day grows colder.

Already the cart-tracks are stiff and red
Pointing like chapped fingers from the gate.
Above the perfunctory grass a level
Eye-flight off, look, close, rigid
A hawk, irate as a stone, with the squireen's cavil.

The flower's eye narrows, pupil-cold
To the master-pinion, nemesis over the heath.
A handful of lambs new-born and hardly
Able to stand or knuckle herd appalled
Underneath. The span grows in the wind more lordly.

A nearby elm gives a warning creak.
The wind is stronger. Cruel, nonchalant
The grown spanshadow ascends, breasting
In smaller and smaller spirals, beak
Proper and cloudgallant, the black land cresting.

Out of terror only a speck that drives
Quickly before the wind to the shoulder line.
The tracks of the kingdom watch and the hammer
Stops under the hill. Each lamb unshrives
His fellow and fine the day is with a laverock shimmer.

Argyle Street

A man with a blowlamp clambers opposite
Burning the brown paint off the sills.
The house in chancery fills
The drab street with indecision, and tonight
Even the corgis at numbers two and twenty-seven
Cannot decide to fight. The mainspring
Seems to be loosed in so many wills
At once. A gull on the tufted chimney
Shrills in the tedious light. Across the haven
The hooters sound, and in them work
Deflates, the semblance of plan and the conscious skills.
A question is posed
And not answered. Why
When so much is ended do we still begin?

The man
With the blowlamp has no use for the dark.
The door of the house in chancery is closed.

For Warren Davies, Two Years Dead

How best remember? Shipwright you, quiet, wry
As a hawk, a viking-cast dropped out of conquest,
Averse from talk when there were gabbers by
And jawed like Magnus at the holocaust.
A crab for history, though, that reared you hard
Where South Hook breaks its point and the pock
Of the fields begins. What was to guard
There but your elders' shins, the proud stock
Of last year's swedes? Better to caulk
And hammer, a foot for each element. Better yet
Rashly, the sun-glimmer white on the stalk
Of cliff wheat, to bolt the herring-set
And sail from Hakin Point into a safer parish
To find a wife. Supple the marriage bond,
Penultimate as life: suddenly it was your wish
To swear out of fervour certainty, terrible and fond.

One of your feet on shore at little cost.
And so, alive in both, to a jig royal in the crowded yard
Chathamward, big with craft. Not grounded, tossed
On the shingle yet, nor ringed up at the hard,
Your Pater tackle held, the homing breeze aroused
A spinnaker, blew the repeat softly on a tack
Up Church Street. Something to be housed,
You thought and grateful, little to lack
With wife and chapel and garden, the chief
Of goods at will. And so, humbly, moods
Notwithstanding, at number twenty-three life
With its print of sixty years began, its crowds
And sermons and keels. A sight of the water
At Lewis Street bottom, mud as they meet,
The trickling pill and the tide, a daughter
In the wake of two sons, and the breathless feat
Of roses running their course narrowly
Between back walls, these pricked your quiet
Like joys. And, upon a time in summer, slowly
Making to ebb, a trick or two with a boat, and by it
Lawrenny smoking across the tide, a plat,
A temporality of grass left rulerless
In trees. Of all your drift of seconds, these that
You cupped from Cleddau were the last to pass.

You rarely wrote. I am your remembrancer.
Your sort of speaking, though, I cannot snatch
Delicately out of the plain pewed answer
Of meeting. You were no Sunday catch
For clowns observant, no plotter had you cold
As sweat under his armpit, waiting for the drop.
If words were a trap sometimes, sometimes your hold
On them slacker than theirs on you, the prop
Of conscience kept your talking up, some little-wanted
Truth tripped out whatever the great boning jaw
Ungripped and said. No man took you for granted
Who had not bought his bed and licked its straw.

The corner after chapel was our beat,
White-collar jobbers and casuists but for you
Who, twice the age of reason, could defeat
A joke like a friend, and hullabaloo
Break on my chest, cracking in jaw

And context with the best. Shake, shake
In the fingers as you did and claw
Sadly at seedlings you were wont to take
Tenderly, this week the clematis
With which you set our hill court in purple
Twice is page again, and up to the lattice
Creeps. How slip, how preening cast of yours, can it recouple
This switch of land to you and greenly in it
Grapple your ailing hand?
                              It was cold,
Cold of a Sunday morning early in Church Street
When you turned in your sleep, and old
Morning, at last unmanned, curtained his gold.

Freshwater West

Over, break white and wash swiftly
Around this rock where earlier
Suds sand hiding swish and uncover.
Press, press on the slope of glass
Sliding over, over. White and pass
Me, wish peace and deliver
From hope, all you byegones, hush
And recover. Break ground and foam
Over and over, newcomers, beat
And surround, beat and surround
And repeat ad finitum, everyone
Beat till the few and the best of these summers
Of mine are as sand, over
And many and meaningless, far beyond
Hand and all measure, lost whereunder
Danger and no man's cast discover.

Wish. I am hidden already. Have I
A wish? Only for peace in the sudden
Hillock of glass and the green
Lease of the tide. Pass,
Pass on your way, over and over,

Beat and digress and repeat, young
Diver and mass old-white
With frays, press and retreat and recover:
Of your half wish there is nothing lost,
Nothing of praise and success, over
And over spoken, nothing but gland
And flesh, a rushing atomiser
Broken like sand from off the human coast.

Searching Spring

Gravelgreat are the hills and perching
Walls are haggard over pitted ground:
In the red manner of a gash the lurching
Streams collide, leaving shoulders ragged
And sudden like the edge
Of our disaster and grave wound. Boulders
Like roofs are lifted off our talk:
Bushes that ruff the hedge and clothe our seeming
Crack in the night and the strained teeming
Multitude of roots sticks in the sight.
No measure now of things that stalk
And vein the sick flayed province under boots:
I had no notion till the fork dug in
My chiefest covenant was with my skin.

Craswall

With a long stirrup under fern
From a small blast of oaks and thorn
The shepherd scours the circling hill
And the sharp dingle creeping to the well.

A trickle from the canting neck
A pony coughing in the track
Are all the stranger hears, and steep
Among the fern the threading of the sheep.

This is the boundary: different burrs
Stick, stones make darker scars
On the road down: nightingales
Struggle with thorn-trees for the gate of Wales.

For an Unmarked Grave

It was night at last when he grew weak
And his chest moved him involuntarily
About the pallet. Night too when the whim
Came to corpse him in tussock
And ramping weed. His bones did not need
Much holding, but the hard-tack joke
Racked up like sputum with the cough
Will take more than the clamping mud off
An upland clod or two, more than the sport
Of October wind, to kill it.

I will speak to him here, in Cwmcamlais ground,
The mountains spare and grudging his time
Against their own. How long is it,
David, long since your loins were water,
Since you were carpenter, wed, kept shop,
Were poor and a theologian, companied
A nephew wide over Senni and the nearer
Hill of day? Nothing to tell,
No fossil couplet, no borrowed stone crying
The claim of a life against an era?
You are not worth a second in the slow
Hardening of Wales, only in the sand
Of the fallen cliff that was my youth.

Departure in Middle Age

The hedges are dazed as cock-crow, heaps of leaves
Brushed back to them like a child's hair
After a sweat, and clouds as recently bundled
Out of the hollows whimper a little in the conifers 'higher up.
I am the one without tears, cold
And strange to myself as a stepfather encountered
For the first time in the passage from the front door.

But I cannot go back, plump up the pillow and shape
My sickness like courage. I have spent the night in a shiver:
Usk water passing now was a chatter under the Fan
When the first cold came on. They are all dead, all,
Or scattered, father, mother, my pinafore friends,
And the playground's echoes have not waited for my return.
Exile is the parcel I carry, and you know this,
Clouds, when you drop your pretences and the hills clear.

Freshwater West Revisited

After six years this winter has not changed,
Encounter of sea and land, ellipses
Of force that intersect and flow boldly
Into and round each other as though
The air were party to either, *socius*
Only because savage both determine so.

This is no place of secondary forms,
Pretty distractions, heights of cliffs
Or trees, not far-out ships puffing
Irrelevantly of other shores and clashes.
Here the brute combers build the waterhead
And grass girds up the dunes the shock washes.

Away inland one can forget so much,
Ease the elliptical abrasions, bandage, duck,
Sidestep the bull-nosed rushes of a wrong
On right, proffer a parody to the back of it.
This cold October morning lays the action bare:
Sea is, and land, and bloodwreck where they meet.

They Have Not Survived

They have not survived,
That swarthy *cenedl*, struggling out
Of the candled *tallut*, cousins to
Generations of sour hay, evil-looking
Apples and oatmeal porringers.
A quick incontinence of seed
Cried in the barn, a mind to spit
And squat harried the gorse
Into burning, and the melancholy
Rhos burst into plots, as circumscribed
Only as the lean muscle yearning
Carefully for love could lay
Around each house. But of that
Merely a life or two, enough to multiply
Cousins like bloodspots in the wasted
Grass. Then a new swarming, under
An aged queen, before they walked
Their *milgis* over the ragged hill
They ghosted every shift, farming
A memory of that last-seen
Country that was never theirs.
It was not will was lacking then
So much as instinct, a gift
Of seed for their backyard culture,
A grip on the girl who bears.

They have not survived.
Coughing in terraces above
The coal, their doorsteps whitened
And the suds of pride draining
Away down the numbered
Steps to the dole, they denied
Both past and future, willing
No further movement than the rattle
Of phlegm, a last composure
Of limb and attitude.
For this dark cousinhood only I
Can speak. Why am I unlike
Them, alive and jack in office,
Shrewd among the plunderers?

Some Tight-lipped Wave
(for Hugh and Lily Griffiths)

Hearing the news from Idris, hoarse,
An undulant like the underwater telephone,
I sat in the outer hall, still strapped in
My unexploded cabin, feeling your Comet's course
Plummet like bedlam from the polities
Into the sea of ancients beyond Kastellorizon,
Your first and ultimate flight one
Catch of innocents for the Minoan savageries.

Out of my porthole I can dimly see
The house at Slade, hay meadow, spit of wood,
Meeting the sea's slap with a jug of mud,
Happily wait your coming. All will be
Grass and haze as so many times before
Till some tight-lipped wave, beating from Greece,
Ranks past the incoming locals and in a trice
Lands with deadly importance on your shore.

Killed in the bomb explosion
en route for Nicosia 13 October 1967

A Letter from Gwyther Street

This morning, the rain pucker over,
I crossed Barafundle from the sun rocks
To the leaf bank westward. It was fine
And feathery on the uppish wave. My feet
In lifting sand uncover an older
Sun and a captured wind dry-beached a decade
Ago. But this is October, the salted-down
Summer of the deckspar, colloped by sea-
Worms, and the indestructible layabout
Plastic of the child engineer.

This evening, such brief spirit sinking, I visit
Friends. And first to the grave-spit at Llanion

Where Sian, her W.V.S. uniform in full
Fold, pairs her ankle-bones to the town. Is there
A message for Elis, tied to his cot like
An idiot, his delicate features clouded
Towards a bad-weather eye? Or Doc, cooped up
With his leg off? Or Herbie, lopsidedly
Smiling in the front room, omnivorous,
History and egg slapped on unknowing cheek?

My footprints this morning on Barafundle
Went in and out of the wave, the fine sand
Darkening at the tide-touch and, as I looked back,
Not a mark of my passing anywhere, only
Sea eating the whiter sift, creaming mouthfuls
Of stick and hampered stone and memory
Trapped there. What remains of companionship
Cannot reach them now, Herbie and Doc
And Elis. No eye-light flickers and signals
Identification on their already buried beach.

New Lease

It's a dead house, he said. Done for.
Why don't you let it lie?
But the naked ashes cry
In the close wind of this captor
Country, impotent fingers snaked
And spread, making that death punishable
For me, that death punishable.

I come to you, house, like Llifiau
From beyond Bannog, crass
As a Pict and no less
Mercenary, a wanderer with an eye
For walls like yours. Weather
And enemy loose will not command us
Lightly, will not command us.

The ashes will spread brazening fingers
Gloved for the summer nights,
A green for the sleights
Of life and garrison. Eye lingers
Not on this new defiance, nor will glimpse,
Till the season bites, our armour gleaming
At dusk, our armour gleaming.

Harri Webb

Most of the poets in this book reveal in their work nationalism of some kind, even if it is no more than an evident love for and concern about the survival of their country. Harri Webb is, however, the most thoroughly committed to this cause. 'My work,' he has said, 'is unrepentantly nationalistic and I seek no audience outside my own country.' He was born in Swansea on 7 September 1920 and educated at Glanmôr School, Swansea, and Magdalen College, Oxford. He was active in the Welsh Republican Movement and has been a member of Plaid Cymru since 1959. He is at present Chief Librarian at Mountain Ash and lives in Merthyr Tydfil. He began to publish poems in the late 'forties in *Wales* and *Triad* and his collected poems 1950–69 were published by Gwasg Gomer, Llandysul, in 1969 under the title *The Green Desert*.

Harri Webb feels that a poet 'must be a leader'. He has offered a lead to the Welsh nation in several poems, most obviously in 'Israel', where he contrasts Wales unfavourably with the equally small but much more active Israeli nation. The poem begins and ends urgently with the words 'Listen, Wales' and regrets that Wales has found no Maccabeus to lead an active resistance:

> They have switched off Mendelssohn
> And tuned in to Maccabeus.
> The mountains are red with their blood,
> The deserts are green with their seed.

Even in this hortatory poem, however, Harri Webb reveals the wit and capacity for wry self-criticism that give to his nationalism a balance and appeal sadly lacking in that of other writers:

> Who lived by playing the violin
> (A lot better, incidentally
> Than you ever played the harp).

Humour is at its lightest and naughtiest in 'Our Budgie' with its outrageous conclusion:

> This futile bird, it seems to me,
> Would make a perfect Welsh M.P.,

and at its richest in 'Synopsis of the Great Welsh Novel', where he assembles the clichés of many years' novelising into an astonishing, slapstick plot that concludes, drily:

> One is not quite sure
> Whether it is fiction or not.

His cleverest comic poem is the 'pop' *cywydd*, 'Cywydd O Fawl', which, in the manner of Caradoc Evans, thanks the 'Big Heads (Welsh) Arts' Council' for supporting Anglo-Welsh poetry:

> In Cardiff is gold yellow,
> Truth it is and no fable,
> All for bards respectable.

So far we have stressed comedy and satire, and we have done so because we think that this aspect of Harri Webb's work will make the first impact upon his reader. His capacity for profound and serious poetry is not, however, in doubt: 'Dyffryn Woods' shows a lyric power to evoke beauty:

> In perfect equipoise a moment
> Between the green leaf and the brown
> The Dyffryn trees still stand in beauty

and compassion:

> While through the streets of crumbling houses
> The old men crawl with lungs of stone.

'Cilmeri' invokes T. S. Eliot's 'The Waste Land' and 'The Hollow Men' to reinforce and broaden an evocation of the 'desert' in the middle of Wales:

> The slack dunes
> Spread further, inland, the wells turn brackish.

The very fine 'The Stone Face' shows Harri Webb at his best, employing his sense of Welsh history and his love for his country to produce significant and memorable poetry. The stone face discovered at Deganwy and which may represent Llewelyn the Great, is effectively pictured:

102

But this stone face under a broken crown
Is not an impersonal mask of sovereignty;
This is the portrait of a living man,

and leads to a moving evocation of archetypal historical moments and a fine elegy for lost greatness:

The Great Orme shepherds the changing weather,
On Menai's shores the tides and generations
Ebb, grumble and flow; harps and hymns
Sound and fall silent; briefly the dream flares out of the eyes
Then darkness comes again.

Critics have commented on the unevenness and inconsistency of Harri Webb's poetry; at its best it demonstrates profound emotion memorably embodied in simple words and appropriate imagery.

Synopsis of the Great Welsh Novel

Dai K lives at the end of a valley. One is not quite sure
Whether it has been drowned or not. His Mam
Loves him too much and his Dada drinks.
As for his girlfriend Blodwen, she's pregnant. So
Are all the other girls in the village – there's been a Revival.
After a performance of Elijah, the mad preacher
Davies the Doom has burnt the chapel down.
One Saturday night after the dance at the Con Club,
With the Free Wales Army up to no good in the back lanes,
A stranger comes to the village; he is, of course,
God, the well known television personality. He succeeds
In confusing the issue, whatever it is, and departs
On the last train before the line is closed.
The colliery blows up, there is a financial scandal
Involving all the most respected citizens; the Choir
Wins at the National. It is all seen, naturally,
Through the eyes of a sensitive boy who never grows up.
The men emigrate to America, Cardiff and the moon. The girls
Find rich and foolish English husbands. Only daft Ianto
Is left to recite the Complete Works of Sir Lewis Morris
To puzzled sheep, before throwing himself over
The edge of the abandoned quarry. One is not quite sure
Whether it is fiction or not.

Our Budgie

Our budgie lives in a cage of wire
Equipped to please his each desire,
He has a little ladder to climb
And he's up and down it all the time.
And a little mirror in which he peeps
As he utters his self-admiring cheeps,
And two little pink plastic budgie mates
Whom he sometimes loves and sometimes hates.
And a little bell all made of tin
On which he makes a merry din.
Though sometimes, when things aren't going well,
He hides his head inside the bell.
His feathers are a brilliant green
And take most of his time to preen,
His speech is limited and blurred
But he doesn't do badly, for a bird.
And though he can but poorly talk
If you ignore him he'll squawk and squawk
And fly into a fearful rage
And rattle the bars of his pretty cage,
But he won't get out, he'll never try it,
And a cloth on the cage will keep him quiet.

This futile bird, it seems to me,
Would make a perfect Welsh M.P.

P.S. to the above
Despite his repertoire of tricks
Poor budgie died in 1966.

The Antennae of the Race

Radar (although we called it then
R.D.F.) predicted a collision.
Nonsense, said skipper, bloody gogglebox,
Not a ship within miles. Then came

The bang in the dark, the deck dipping
To a sudden scar of white foam,
The long wallowing night, the thin cheer
That rose like a death-wail at dawn
Revealing known faces suddenly strange,
Girlish almost, bright-eyed with fatigue, rouged
By the half gale. All hands, including
The radar crew, Ike, Buck and Les, their box of tricks
Jarred blank, stood by with the collision mat.
We were right after all, they said
As we made it back to the Clyde, patched up,
Sailed on. The bang came
Just as we said it would. The radar, though,
Was buggered. Poets, beware.

Dyffryn Woods
(for Robert Morgan, who asks, from exile, How are the Dyffryn trees now?)

In perfect equipoise a moment
Between the green leaf and the brown
The Dyffryn trees still stand in beauty
About the mean and straggling town.

Last of the spreading woods of Cynon
Our nameless poet loved and sung
Calling a curse on their despoilers
The men of iron heart and tongue.

In stillness at the end of autumn
They wait to see the doom fulfilled,
The final winter of the townships
When the last pithead wheels are stilled.

Our earth, though plundered to exhaustion
Still has the strength to answer back,
In houses built above the workings
The roof trees sag, the hearth stones crack.

Soon the last truckload down the valley
Will leave the sidings overgrown
While through the streets of crumbling houses
The old men crawl with lungs of stone.

And now as in the long green ages
The Dyffryn trees stand full and tall,
As lovely as in exile's memory,
Breathless, a breath before the fall.

Cywydd O Fawl
(yn null y gogogynfeirdd à gogo)

Flap we our lips, praise Big Man,
Bards religious shire Cardigan.
Not frogs croaking are we
Nor vain crows are bards tidy.
Wise is our speak, like Shadrach,
Hearken you now, people *bach*.
Mouth some, Cardiff *ach y fi*,
Not holy like Aberteifi.
Twp it is to speech so,
In Cardiff is gold yellow,
Truth it is and no fable,
All for bards respectable.
White Jesus *bach*, let no ill
Befall Big Heads Arts Council.
Pounds they have, many thousand,
Like full till shop draper grand.
Good is the work they are at,
Soaped they shall be in Seiat,
Reserved shall be for them
A place in big seat Salem.
Praised let them be for this thing,
Money they are distributing
Like Beibil Moses his manna,
Tongue we all, bards Welsh, Ta!

Cilmeri

In the nameless years shapeless as sand dunes
Oblivion drifted over Aberffraw, the foursided grave
On the banks of the Alaw gave up the dust of Branwen
But the stone coffins rang empty of the bones
Of fallen princes, dead principalities.
The hall brought from Conway to the hold
Of the stone battleship moored below Segontium
Is unaccounted for. An ignorant past
Careless of its idiot plunder, spendthrift
Even of David's Sapphire and the Croes Naidd
Has squandered our treasure, bestowed on harlotry
The wages of our blood, sold in the market place
The decent things of our people for beer and beads.

So we have come to this. There is nothing left
Tangible, no way of speech or thought or song
That is valid any more. There is only death, ours,
The nation's, and all the deaths for her sake.
So we have come to this stone. In the time
Of yellow grass, no flowers, iron earth. So
We have come.

Here is only stone, water and death.
In a dead season. There is no guarantee
That anything will come of this; no sacrament
Is valid any more. The slack dunes
Spread further, inland, the wells turn brackish
Or dry up. Here in the heart of the hills
Where the strategic roads converged to crucify:
A stone, water, words.

In the cold air the words fall like stones
In water: a splash, a ripple of rings,
A brief erosion. But the echo rouses
The sleeping augural birds, and suddenly
The sky is full of wings.

Israel

Listen, Wales. Here was a people
Whom even you could afford to despise,
Growing nothing, making nothing,
Belonging nowhere, a people
Whose sweat-glands had atrophied,
Who lived by their wits,
Who lived by playing the violin
(A lot better, incidentally
Than you ever played the harp).
And because they were such a people
They went like lambs to the slaughter.

But some survived (yes, listen closer now)
And these are a different people,
They have switched off Meldelssohn
And tuned in to Maccabeus.
The mountains are red with their blood,
The deserts are green with their seed.
Listen, Wales.

In Memory of Harri Jones

From Irfon, guilty water
And up the Chwefri where
A dead prince and a dead poet
Called me, the road leads
From Epynt where all words
Fail in the witless wind.
You did well to get out of
This hole in the middle of Wales,
Only there is nowhere else
Anywhere. I went on:
Dylife, broken teeth
Snarling, Clywedog, a wound
Laying bare the black Silurian
Bedrock of rotten bone.
Were you perhaps lucky
Not to come back to this land
Of dead villages and ruined harvests?

The Stone Face
(discovered at Deganwy, Spring 1966)

It may of course be John his father-in-law,
Their worst, our best not easily discernible
After so many buried centuries. The experts
Cannot be sure, that is why they are experts.
But this stone face under a broken crown
Is not an impersonal mask of sovereignty;
This is the portrait of a living man
And when his grandson burnt Deganwy down
So that no foreign army should hold its strength
I think they buried the head of Llywelyn Fawr
As primitive magic and for reasons of state.

No fortress was ever destroyed so utterly
As was Deganwy by Llywelyn the Last,
The thoroughness of despair, foreknown defeat,
Was in the burning and breaking of its walls.
But at some door or window a hand paused,
A raised crowbar halted by the stare
Of a stone face. The Prince is summoned
And the order given: bury it in the earth,
There will be other battles, we'll be back –
Spoken in the special Welsh tone of voice
Half banter, half blind fervour, the last look
Exchanged between the hunted living eyes
And the dead majesty for whom there are no problems.

The burning of Deganwy, the throne and fortress
Of Llywelyn Fawr shattered, his principality
Gone in the black smoke drifting over Menai
And his last heir forced into endless retreat.
To the banks of Irfon and the final lance-thrust.
There was no return, no reverent unearthing.
A stone face sleeps beneath the earth
With open eyes. All history is its dream.
The Great Orme shepherds the changing weather,
On Menai's shores the tides and generations
Ebb, grumble and flow; harps and hymns
Sound and fall silent; briefly the dream flares out of the eyes
Then darkness comes again.

Seven hundred and fifty years of darkness.
Now in a cold and stormy spring we stand
At the unearthing of the Sovereign head,
The human face under the chipped crown.
Belatedly, but not too late, the rendezvous is made,
The dream and the inheritors of the dream,
The founder and father, and those who must rebuild
The broken fortresses, re-established the throne
Of eagles, here exchange the gaze of eagles
In the time of the cleansing of the eyes.

Leslie Norris

Leslie Norris was born in Merthyr Tydfil on 21 May 1921. Merthyr, though an industrial town, lies close to the Brecon Beacons National Park, so that in 'Water' we see children gaining 'the enormous experience of the mountain'. Another side of Merthyr produces poems like 'An Evening by the Lake', set in Cyfarthfa Park, and 'The Ballad of Billy Rose', which evokes the boxing traditions of the town. His childhood and youth in Merthyr are an important source of this poet's inspiration.

He began to write poetry at an early age, and after leaving school served in the R.A.F., out of which he was invalided in 1940, just before the publication of his first short collection of poems. For a time he worked in the Borough Treasurer's department in Merthyr, before preparing, at Coventry Training College and the University of Southampton, for a career in teaching. In the early 'forties he published two pamphlets of poetry in the *Resurgam Younger Poets* series put out by the Favil Press. The first, *Tongue of Beauty*, appeared in his 22nd year; the second, *Poems*, in 1946. In 1948 he joined the staff of Bognor Regis College of Education where he worked until recently.

After his early writing and publication of poetry in the 'forties, he wrote little and published nothing for about fourteen years (in this respect he resembles John Ormond). Creativity was resumed in about 1964, and in 1967 *The Loud Winter* was published in the *Triskel Poets* series and *Finding Gold* by Chatto. *Ransoms* was published by the same firm in 1970 and won the Alice Hunt Bartlett Award of the Poetry Society. His latest volume, also from Chatto, is *Mountains, Polecats, Pheasants* (1974).

The stimulus for his renewed creative activity in 1964 seems to have been the rediscovery and revaluation, by a poet living far from his home area, of the experiences of childhood and youth. 'An Evening by the Lake' typically begins with a visit to the town in which he has

111

not lived 'for twenty years', and its relaxed, colloquial tone is characteristic:

> Well, let us admit it, I make
> A pleasant picture here. A check
> Overcoat, fresh from the cleaners,
> Discreet suede shoes.

This develops, however, into an almost Wordsworthian account of an incident from the poet's youth which leaves him in a very different posture:

> So that I stand alone and
> Bowed, on a scuffed, gravel path, in
> A shabby park, my legs tired, my
> Heart shaken

robbed of his jaunty self-confidence and conscious of his age. Similar inspiration produces 'Gardening Gloves':

> I remember my father's hands,
> How they moved as mine do now,

'Water', with its beautiful evocation of summer:

> Softly, leaning, their sleepy faces warm for home.
> We would see them murmur slowly through our stiff
> Gate, their shy heads gilded by the last sun,

(rather sentimentalised, perhaps), and 'Early Frost', which is certainly not sentimental and has impressive, painful reality:

> I ran through the bitterness on legs
> That might have been brittle, my breath
> Solid, grasping at stabs of bleak
> Pain to gasp on.

Another aspect, urban and brutal, is seen in 'The Ballad of Billy Rose':

> I had forgotten that day
> As if it were dead for ever, yet now I saw
> The flowers of punched blood on the ring floor,
> As bright as his name.

Leslie Norris is a careful writer who revises his work extensively, and an experimental craftsman, using free verse and invented forms which are, however, patterned and shaped by assonance and alliteration (e.g. 'Gardening Gloves'). His capacity for exact description, particularly of the natural scene, is evident in 'Early Frost':

                Late
        Bees hung their blunt weight,
        Plump drops between those simplest wings . . .

though he evokes with equal clarity stones, the 'Mild, knob-jointed,
old' gardening gloves, and the bridge:

                its one foot
        Clamped hard on bedrock, and such grace
        In its growth it resembles flying.

With this vivid concreteness as foundation, his poetry functions power-
fully to engage emotion, stimulate thought and convince the reader of
the reality and relevance of his achievement.

        An Evening by the Lake

        Well, let us admit it, I make
        A pleasant picture here. A check
        Overcoat, fresh from the cleaners,
        Discreet suede shoes, (I use a wire brush),
        Trouser-legs, that new bronze-green colour,
        Just narrow enough for good taste.
        I walk briskly, waving now and then and
        Gently, a tweed hat.
        Even my dog, unfashionable but
        Successful, adds to my satisfaction.
        She is obedient, but not servile.
        On this grey evening, here at the edge
        Of the lake and under the clouds,
        She skips on the washed grass and is
        Complacently white.
                              I have not lived
        In the town for twenty years.

        But walked this lakeside drive four times
        A day when a boy, going to school
        In a comic Gothic castle, built
        For a fat iron-master. It turns
        A stolid, limestone gaze down at
        Me now.

The park is quite deserted,
But for some poor boys, younger
Than I was, playing a thoughtless
Game a long way off. I watch them
Lift a great dressed stone, from
An old wall perhaps, stagger the few
Uneven yards to the water,
Then drop the huge thing in. I see
The little fountain of its drowning,
Then the slow circles spread. Boys' voices
Bounce to me over the resilient water.
Later I hear the stone's loud splash,
Much later.

      Four of us on this lake,
Using two boats, once rowed for the price
Of their hire a furious race. Off
To a gasped start, we plunged our oars
For all our thin arms' worth,
Driving the clumsy prows through
Burst reflections of the full clouds
And green banks. When I lifted my
Dripping blade from the water, (Dan
Chanting our time), I could see behind
The lovely dimpling of its leaving
The liquid skin.

      Then at last we stopped,
And called, our high voices skidding
Like flat, thrown stones over the resonant
Surface.

      Just like these later voices,
And this younger water, which have
Entered the locked cellar of my mind,
Broken its seal, and let its darkness
Out.

      So that I stand alone and
Bowed, on a scuffed, gravel path, in
A shabby park, my legs tired, my
Heart shaken, my jaunty clothes all
Wrong. All right, so my youth is dead.
And yes, those boys are gone.

The Ballad of Billy Rose

Outside Bristol Rovers' Football Ground –
The date has gone from me, but not the day,
Nor how the dissenting flags in stiff array
Struck bravely out against the sky's grey round –

Near the Car Park then, past Austin and Ford,
Lagonda, Bentley, and a colourful patch
Of country coaches come in for the match,
Was where I walked, having travelled the road

From Fishponds to watch Portsmouth in the Cup.
The Third Round, I believe. And I was filled
With the old excitement which had thrilled
Me so completely when, while growing up,

I went on Saturdays to match or fight.
Not only me; for thousands of us there
Strode forward eagerly, each man aware
Of tingling memory, anticipating delight.

We all marched forward, all, except one man.
I saw him because he was paradoxically still,
A stone against the flood, face upright against us all,
Head bare, hoarse voice aloft, blind as a stone.

I knew him at once, despite his pathetic clothes;
Something in his stance, or his sturdy frame
Perhaps. I could even remember his name
Before I saw it on his blind-man's tray. Billy Rose.

And twenty forgetful years fell away at the sight.
Bare-kneed, dismayed, memory fled to the hub
Of Saturday violence, with friends to the Labour Club,
Watching the boxing on a sawdust summer night.

The boys' enclosure close to the shabby ring
Was where we stood, clenched in a resin world,
Spoke in cool voices, lounged, were artificially bored
During minor bouts. We paid threepence to go in.

Billy Rose fought there. He was top of the bill.
So brisk a fighter, so gallant, so precise!
Trim as a tree he stood for the ceremonies,
Then turned to meet George Morgan of Tirphil.

He had no chance. Courage was not enough,
Nor tight defence. Donald Davies was sick
And we threatened his cowardice with an embarrassed kick.
Ripped across both his eyes was Rose, but we were tough

And clapped him as they wrapped his blindness up
In busy towels, applauded the wave
He gave his executioners, cheered the brave
Blind man as he cleared with a jaunty hop

The top rope. I had forgotten that day
As if it were dead for ever, yet now I saw
The flowers of punched blood on the ring floor,
As bright as his name. I do not know

How long I stood with ghosts of the wild fists
And the cries of shaken boys long dead around me,
For struck to act at last, in terror and pity
I threw some frantic money, three treacherous pence –

And I cry at the memory – into his tray, and ran,
Entering the waves of the stadium like a drowning man.
Poor Billy Rose. God, he could fight,
Before my three sharp coins knocked out his sight.

Gardening Gloves

Mild, knob-jointed, old,
They lie on the garage floor.
Scarred by the turn of a spade
In hard, agricultural wear
And soiled by seasonal mould
They *look* like animal skins –
Or imagine a gargoyle's hands.

But not my hands I'd swear,
Being large, rough and uncouth;
Yet the moment I pick them up
They assume an absurd truth,
They assert I have given them shape,
Making my hands the mirror
For their comfortable horror.

And I know if I put them on
I gain a deliberate skill,
An old, slow satisfaction
That is not mine at all
But sent down from other men.
Yes, dead men live again
In my reluctant skin.

I remember my father's hands,
How they moved as mine do now
While he took his jokes from the air
Like precise, comical birds.
These gloves are my proper wear.
We all preserve such lives.
I'm not sorry to have these gloves.

Water

On hot summer mornings my aunt set glasses
On a low wall outside the farmhouse,
With some jugs of cold water.
I would sit in the dark hall, or
          Behind the dairy window,
Waiting for children to come from the town.

They came in small groups, serious, steady,
And I could see them, black in the heat,
Long before they turned in at our gate
To march up the soft, dirt road.
          They would stand by the wall,
Drinking water with an engrossed thirst. The dog

Did not bother them, knowing them responsible
Travellers. They held in quiet hands their bags
Of jam sandwiches, and bottles of yellow fizz.
Sometimes they waved a gratitude to the house,
               But they never looked at us.
Their eyes were full of the mountain, lifting

Their measuring faces above our long hedge.
When they had gone I would climb the wall,
Looking for them among the thin sheep runs.
Their heads were a resolute darkness among ferns,
               They climbed with unsteady certainty.
I wondered what it was they knew the mountain had.

They would pass the last house, Lambert's, where
A violent gander, too old by many a Christmas,
Blared evil warning from his bitten moor,
Then it was open world, too high and clear
               For clouds even, where over heather
The free hare cleanly ran, and the summer sheep.

I knew this; and I knew all summer long
Those visionary gangs passed through our lanes,
Coming down at evening, their arms full
Of cowslips, moon daisies, whinberries, nuts,
               All fruits of the sliding seasons,
And the enormous experience of the mountain

That I who loved it did not understand.
In the summer, dust filled our winter ruts
With a level softness, and children walked
At evening through golden curtains scuffed
               From the road by their trailing feet.
They would drink tiredly at our wall, talking

Softly, leaning, their sleepy faces warm for home.
We would see them murmur slowly through our stiff
Gate, their shy heads gilded by the last sun.
One by one we would gather up the used jugs,
               The glasses. We would pour away
A little water. It would lie on the thick dust, gleaming.

Early Frost

We were warned about frost, yet all day the summer
Has wavered its heat above the empty stubble. Late
Bees hung their blunt weight,
Plump drops between those simplest wings, their leisure
An ignorance of frost.
My mind is full of the images of summer
And a liquid curlew calls from alps of air;

But the frost has come. Already under trees
Pockets of summer are dying, wide paths
Of the cold glow clean through the stricken thickets
And again I feel on my cheek the cut of winters
Dead. Once I awoke in a dark beyond moths
To a world still with freezing,
Hearing my father go to the yard for his ponies,

His hands full of frostnails to point their sliding
To a safe haul. I went to school,
Socks pulled over shoes for the streets' clear glass,
The early shops cautious, the tall
Classroom windows engraved by winter's chisel,
Fern, feather and flower that would not let the pale
Day through. We wrote in a cold fever for the morning

Play. Then boys in the exulting yard, ringing
Boots hard on winter, slapped with their polishing
Caps the arrows of the gliding, in steaming lines
Ran till they launched one by one
On the skills of ice their frail balance,
Sliding through life with not a fall in mind,
Their voices crying freely through such shouting

As the cold divided. I slid in the depth
Of the season till the swung bell sang us in.
Now insidious frost, its parched grains rubbing
At crannies, moved on our skin.
Our fingers died. Not the warmth
Of all my eight wide summers could keep me smiling.
The circle of the popping stove fell still
And we were early sped through the hurrying dark.

I ran through the bitterness on legs
That might have been brittle, my breath
Solid, grasping at stabs of bleak
Pain to gasp on. Winter branched in me, ice cracked
In my bleeding. When I fell through the teeth
Of the cold at my haven door I could not see

For locked tears, I could not feel the spent
Plenty of flames banked at the range,
Nor my father's hands as they roughed the blue
Of my knees. But I knew what he meant
With the love of his rueful laugh, and my true
World unfroze in a flood of happy crying,
As hot on my cheek as the sting of this present

Frost. I have stood too long in the orderly
Cold of the garden. I would not have again the death
Of that day come unasked as the comfortless dusk
Past the stakes of my fences. Yet these are my
Ghosts, they do not need to ask
For housing when the early frost comes down.
I take them in, all, to the settled warmth.

Stones

On the flat of the earth lie
Stones, their eyes turned
To earth's centre, always.
If you throw them they fly
Grudgingly, measuring your arm's
Weak curve before homing
To a place they know.

Digging, we may jostle
Stones with our thin tines
Into stumbling activity.
Small ones move most.
When we turn from them
They grumble to a still place.
It can take a month to grate

That one inch. Watch how stones
Clutter together on hills
And beaches, settling heavily
In unremarkable patterns.
A single stone can vanish
In a black night, making
Someone bury it in water.

We can polish some;
Onyx, perhaps, chalcedony,
Jasper and quartzite from
The edges of hard land.
But we do not alter them.
Once in a million years
Their stone hearts lurch.

A True Death
(for Vernon Watkins 1906–1967)

When summer is dead, when evening
October is dying, the pendulum
Heart falters, and the firm
Blood hangs its drops in a swing
Of stone. Laughing, we catch breath
Again. But his was the true death

Our rehearsals imitate. I lived
On the charred hills where industrial
Fires for a hundred years had grieved
All things growing. On still,
On the stillest days, a burnish
Of sea glinted at the world's edge

And died with the sun. There
Were twenty miles of Wales between
My streams and the water lore
He knew. He watched the green
Passages of the sea, how it rides
The changing, unchanging roads

Of its hollowing power. Caves
From his flooded cliffs called to him,
Dunes with their harsh grasses
Sang, the river-mouths spoke of home
In Carmarthen hills. Small stones
Rang like bells, touching his hands.

Last year we sat in his garden,
Quietly, in new wooden chairs,
Grasshoppers rasped on the hot lawn.
Shadows gathered at his shoulders
As he spoke of the little tormentil,
Tenacious flower; growing there still.

Stone and Fern

It is not that the sea lanes
Are too long, nor that I am not
Tempted by the birds' sightless

Roads, but that I have listened
Always to the voice of the stone,
Saying: Sit still, answer, say

Who you are. And I have answered
Always with the rooted fern,
Saying: We are the dying seed.

Bridges

Imagine the bridge launched, its one foot
Clamped hard on bedrock, and such grace
In its growth it resembles flying, is flight
Almost. It is not chance when they speak
Of throwing a bridge; it leaves behind a track
Of its parallel rise and fall, solid
In quarried stone, in timber, in milled
Alloy under stress. A bridge is

The path of flight. A friend, a soldier,
Built a laughable wartime bridge over
Some unknown river. In featureless night
He threw from each slid bank the images
Of his crossing, working in whispers, under
Failing lamps. As they built, braced spars,
Bolted taut the great steel plugs, he hoped
His bridge would stand in brawny daylight, complete,

The two halves miraculously knit. But
It didn't. Airily they floated above
Midstream, going nowhere, separate
Beginnings of different bridges, offering
The policies of inaction, neither coming
Nor going. His rough men cursed, sloped off,
Forded quite easily a mile lower.
It was shallow enough for his Land Rover.

I have a bridge over a stream. Four
Wooden sleepers, simple, direct. After rain,
Very slippery. I rarely cross right over,
Preferring to stand, watching the grain
On running water. I like such bridges best,
River bridges on which men always stand,
In quiet places. Unless I could have that other,
A bridge launched, hovering, wondering where to land.

Harri Jones

Thomas Henry Jones was a Breconshire man, thoroughly Welsh yet, like many Breconshire people, unable to speak the language. He was born in 1921 at Llanafan Fawr, where, he said, his family had been established for more than three hundred years.

He began to write poetry while he was at school and continued to do so during his war service in mine-sweepers in the Mediterranean. His first poems were published during this time. After the War he studied English at University College, Aberystwyth, from which he graduated with First Class Honours. He gained an M.A. in 1950.

In 1959, after teaching in London and Portsmouth, he emigrated with his wife and three daughters to Australia, where he lectured at Newcastle University College, New South Wales. He was very popular with his colleagues and with his students, being a successful lecturer and enthusiastic reader of poetry. He gained a reputation for his poetry readings.

There are four volumes of his poetry, all published by Rupert Hart-Davis. Three were published during his lifetime – *The Enemy in the Heart* (1957); *Songs of a Mad Prince* (1960) and *The Beast at the Door* (1963). The fourth, *The Colour of Cockcrowing*, was published posthumously in 1966. Harri Jones was drowned at Newcastle, New South Wales, on 29 January 1965.

'Of course, we Welshmen are exiles,' he says in 'Mr Jones as the Transported Poet' and in 'Back', significantly dedicated to R. S. Thomas, he speaks bitterly about the circumstances that make exile necessary to so many of the most creative of Welsh artists. Though separated from 'my mind's country' he writes much poetry that is specifically concerned with Welsh life and landscape.

His naval experience during the Second World War is reflected in the important part that the sea and sea-imagery play in his poetry. 'Sailor' portrays a man for whom

Remembered tides at once roar in his ears
And ride him down beneath his frightened eyes.

124

'Here is the peace of the fathers' is, sadly, prophetic of his own death

> Requite in all green undertows
> The bitter overtones
> Of my unpeaceful bones.

Though the titles of his published volumes are colourful, romantic
and reminiscent of, or even quoted from, Dylan Thomas, Harri Jones
is a conscious, experimental artist for whom the intellect is certainly
no less important than the emotions. He was influenced by and to
some extent resembles W. H. Auden, the most 'modern' and experimental of British twentieth-century poets. 'The Pride of the Morning'
is like Auden's 'As I Walked Out One Evening' and Harri Jones' liking
for different forms and styles can be seen in poems like the sestina
'It Is Not Fear'. Though his roots are firmly in Wales and Welsh
culture, his poetry is cosmopolitan. 'Critical Encounter' shows a self-
conscious, sardonic awareness:

> The poem still remains.
> Now that I read it in a different light,
> (How cunningly I picked the fellow's brains!)
> I could so easily believe him right . . .

that distinguishes him from many of the poets in this anthology.

More than most other poets here he is concerned about passionate, sexual love. His awareness of its power and disturbance is seen
most clearly in 'Girl Reading John Donne', its overmastering delight
in 'Adam's Song After Paradise'. In 'The Beast At the Door' he stresses
its danger, especially to 'civilised' man,

> I was ready to welcome it
> Until I knew those white
> Fangs were for me, and shut
> The door, too late, too late.

Linked, naturally, with this is his concern about old age and death. In
'A Promise to My Old Age' he wrote what we could accept as his
epitaph:

> blame or thank or curse or praise
> This earlier brash hero if you must.
> Only remember here his promise lies.

Harri Jones might well have become one of the best of the modern
Anglo-Welsh poets; he was undoubtedly one of the most promising.

The Pride of the Morning

As I walked out in the pride of the morning,
  Too young to admire and too old to deride,
I saw the whole city was bonny with fire
  And everyone else had suddenly died.

So I walked for a while in the pride of the morning,
  Alone, with a strut, and a dandified smile,
The king of the fire, the lord of the city,
  Flamboyant, alone, and proud for a while.

But alas for the dandy, alas for the king,
  Alas for the pride that is nourished on fire,
The flames as I passed them were courteous with homage
  But my heart wanted someone to see and admire.

My heart shrivelled up in the pride of the morning,
  Played traitor, alas, to the dandy and king,
Because I was walking alone in my splendour
  And the fire was deaf to the song I could sing.

Critical Encounter

This critic was too subtle is my guess.
  I was dismayed at first, but later thought
His ambiguities concerned me less
  Than the cold comfort that my poem brought.

Not that I'd trust entirely my own wit
  To tell me what I mean by every word.
Doubtless he's right when he untangles it –
  But then I have a sense of the absurd.

Would it have made any difference
  If I'd disclaimed responsibility?
No. For the critic must have confidence –
  The poet makes do with fallibility.

So we agreed at last to separate,
    And go our ways, and try to understand.
We did not make our gestures desperate –
    Just smiled, and shook each other by the hand.

And left. The poem still remains.
    Now that I read it in a different light,
(How cunningly I picked the fellow's brains!)
    I could so easily believe him right.

It Is Not Fear

It is not fear but knowing what to fear
Frightens you most, whatever you believe.
I ought to know: I bought the knowledge dear.

You will find out, this or some other year,
In saying this I don't mean to deceive:
It is not fear but knowing what to fear.

And when my meaning's made completely clear,
You will of course have further cause to grieve.
I ought to know: I bought the knowledge dear.

And then you shall regret the shrug and sneer
With which you take this warning I must give:
It is not fear but knowing what to fear.

I give the warning now because you're near
And I must try to tell you how to live –
I ought to know: I bought the knowledge dear.

And even though you still refuse to hear
The warning or claim your right to disbelieve:
It is not fear but knowing what to fear.
I ought to know: I bought the knowledge dear.

Sailor

Easy now on a beach, he notes the sea
(An old bitch once, angry to bite and keep)
As over-emphatic in vulgarity;
And turns upon his side prepared to sleep.

Remembered tides at once roar in his ears
And ride him down beneath his frightened eyes.
Scrabble and gasp among the plunging fears
Betray the nonchalance with which he lies.

Easy on whatever harmless shore
The green ghost will not lightly let him be.
His blood cannot forget the salty roar,
The suck and gobble of the feeding sea.

Saltsick, seadriven, he abdicates his right
To be at ease with his old enemy.
Witness the longdrawn watches of the night
He drowns again in a remembered sea.

A Promise To My Old Age

Strut, arrogant frame, your pride of bones
Over this green stage while the sun is shining.
When the sag comes and your now so limber lines
Begin to blur and creak, and the complaining
Breath annoys the air your movements cumber,
Then you shall with no regret remember
How you, lordly, strode earth once
Like any rightful owner, and were pleased
To see tall trees reflect your arrogance,
And knew that nothing young could be despised.

Old age, my fatal friend I do not know,
Remember, when some young itch interferes
With your anticipated peace, I pray
Your freedom from these terrors and desires

Of disobedient flesh, and promise pride
Only in glories that have long been dead.
Whatever song or madness your last lust
May farrow, blame or thank or curse or praise
This earlier brash hero if you must.
Only remember here his promise lies.

Adam's Song After Paradise
(to A. D. Hope)

And I remember how I named
The innocent beasts that came to me
And God said what I did was good
And for reward created thee
Torn from my side and fashioned fair
To be my hope and my despair.

How I have lapsed from innocence
Since first we lay and were as one
So that we now do furtively
The deed in open joy begun
And beg the favour of the night
To cover us from our delight.

And shall I blame thee? shall I blame
Seductiveness of hair and eyes
The promised welcome of your breasts
And long allurements of your thighs,
Say these are blazons of my shame
And know the heartbreak of your name?

I take again your guilty hand
I look into your candid eyes
And am content that I have lost
That half-regretted Paradise
To win your human smiles and tears
To comfort my declining years.

The Beast At The Door
(to Brin)

When the beast came to the door,
Amiably slavering, his paw
Uplifted as in salute,
I noted the burrs on his coat,
And the small thorns that clung
To the wilful clots of dung
He wore like medals, felt
The sweat reek from his pelt,
His friendly stinking breath,
My knees bent therewith;
For all his looming size,
And his incongruous eyes
Small as a pig's, or mine,
I would have him as my own,
Blatantly in my house,
Bald-rumped, big-pilled, wise
To smell out my tricks
As he sniffed around for sex
Or murdered meat,
Mauled what he would not eat.
When the beast came to the door,
Ambiguous visitor,
Expected and casual,
Despite his grin and scowl
I was ready to welcome it
Until I knew those white
Fangs were for me, and shut
The door, too late, too late.

Mr Jones as the Transported Poet
(for Gwen)

'And how do you react to exile?' Politely
They ask; and remnants of my country courtesy
Make me answer politely, meaninglessly.

I say, 'Of course, a poet is in exile
Anywhere, always.' And that 'of course' disarms,
Undoes them. They are politely satisfied
There was something they always knew about poets.

Or I say, putting on a bit more accent,
And of course prefacing what I have to say
With that disarming and dishonest 'of course',
I say, 'Of course, we Welshmen are exiles
Just as much in England as Australia.'
And they nod understandingly and smile politely,
And think I didn't really understand the question.

How could I tell them, politely or impolitely,
That the only exile is from her bed,
From that visionary and impossible moment
When our customary involvement made
A sudden meaning we had not known before?

Exile, like love, is a word not to be lightly said.

Back?
(to R. S. Thomas)

Back is the question
Carried to me on the curlew's wing,
And the strong sides of the salmon.

Should I go back then
To the narrow path, the sheep turds,
And the birded language?

Back to an old, thin bitch
Fawning on my spit, writhing
Her lank belly with memories:

Back to the chapel, and a charade
Of the word of God made by a preacher
Without a tongue:

Back to the ingrowing quarrels,
The family where you have to remember
Who is not speaking to whom:

Back to the shamed memories of Glyn Dwr
And Saunders Lewis's aerodrome
And a match at Swansea?

Of course I'd go back if somebody'd pay me
To live in my own country
Like a bloody Englishman.

But for now, lacking the money,
I must be content with the curlew's cry
And the salmon's taut belly

And the waves, of water and of fern
And words, that beat unendingly
On the rocks of my mind's country.

Girl Reading John Donne

Her arms bare, and her eyes naked,
She tells her borrowed book, *I am in love*,
And the fierce poem jumps about under her skin.

Mr, the almost anonymous lecturer
Who prescribed this text for her undoing,
When he said *Goodmorrow* to his shaving self,
Remembered how she crossed her legs in class,
Thought vaguely of writing a poem, a declaration,
But after breakfast went on marking assignments.

The girl sits blazing in the Library,
Alight over the poem to which she says
I am in love, I am in love. And the poem's
Words flame up to her unseeing eyes.
She does not need to read, only remember
The poem says *I love* to her exposed
And wanted flesh.
                              She reads naked in the Library.

Mr every now and again is deflected
From his marking, boredom, marking time,
To wonder momentarily if he was right
To ask of vulnerable innocence
What it thinks about the imprisonment
Of a great Prince.
                              His automatic pencil,
Cancelling an ampersand, dismisses
The futile question. He feels morally secure
Because he didn't interrogate them,
Her, about her, his favourite Elegie.
At that minding of bed's America
He resolutely goes on marking.
                              It's marking time.

And the naked girl in the Library
Reads a naked poem to herself, and says
I am in love, I am in love, over and over
Until the poem's canicule and sear
Become unbearable, when she burns out
To dissertate over a coke or coffee
On anything, anything except this poem,
This love, bare longing, that bed, this poem.

And elsewhere a great Prince in prison lies.

My Grandfather Going Blind

When the cataracts came down, he remembered
Verses, grew grumpier, but did not cry or break.
His bulk sagged, shrunk a little; he would have liked
The comforting presence of Mari, even as she was
Those last years, tiny woman in a big chair,
Talking mostly to her small boy sons, though
Sometimes she came back to this world for a moment.
When the cataracts came down, he remembered.
Was sometimes peevish, liked to talk in Welsh,
Was for the most part content with his old dog,
Blind, deaf, rheumatic, and pretty daft,
His firm stick, strong pipe, his memories – and me:
His grandson who could not speak his language,
Lacked his mountain skills, but in whom
He had a thorny faith not to be beaten
Down by any wind or language.
When the cataracts came down, creeping
Curtains over his shepherd eyes,
He talked to me.
                        The old names still resound
For me of farms, men, ponies, dogs,
The old names that are all that I possess
Of my own language, proud then
And prouder now to call myself only
Young Crogau, old Crogau's grandson.

I remember when the cataracts came down.

Welsh Childhood

Eating the bread of the world
In the thin rain of time
The child ignores the crow,
The stoat, and worm who know
What bread and child will come
To, crumble to at last.

In comfort on harsh rock
Or lacerated pine,
Never out of the wind
Or the thin nails of rain,
He thinks that wind the breath
Of the world he knows is truth.

A bible in his mind,
A pulpit for his mouth,
Should he seek further for
The absence of the wind
Or accommodating truth,
Life's wound without a scar?

The crow, the stoat, the worm
Wait because they know
He will never be out of the wind,
As long as he has breath,
That breath is the truth
He crumbles to in the end.

Builth Wells

A picture of a town beside a river:
Schoolcaps, girls' knickers, French letters,
And French teachers, beside the sylvan Wye:
How beautifully my memories lie.

Builth, Buallt, spa of no renown,
But sprawled about the grassy Groe,
Along the brawling reaches of the Wye,
Where I'll go home to die:

Small town, home of a great footballer
And of a greater choir, O Builth.
Stay small beside my memoried Wye
Where all my poems lie.

'Here is the Peace of the Fathers'
Hart Crane

Drowned meadows, submarine
Shadows, lapsed bones in the swell,
Old talkers who now talk ghostlily well
Between one green and another green,
How my bones feel that your bones do well.

Peace, fathers, peace.
Talk, and may the peace where your bones dwell
Requite in all green undertows
The bitter overtones
Of my unpeaceful bones.

John Ormond

John Ormond was born at Dunvant, Swansea, in 1923. His father was the village shoemaker:

> Here lies a shoemaker whose knife and hammer
> Fell idle in the height of summer . . .
>
> ('At His Father's Grave')

and many of his relations worked in local coal mines. As we shall see, this early life and its experiences have formed the heart of his inspiration. Like Leslie Norris, he wrote and published poems early and then went through a fallow period before recovering his inspiration. Before he was twenty he had already published poetry in a number of magazines such as *The Poetry Quarterly* and *Wales*, and in 1943 he shared a volume entitled *Indications* with James Kirkup and John Bayliss (published by the Grey Walls Press). His early achievement was such that two of his poems were published in *Modern Welsh Poetry*, edited by Keidrych Rhys in 1944. At this time he was studying philosophy and English at University College, Swansea, and simultaneously cultivating an interest in art and artists that has been almost as important to him as poetry and has influenced the matter and manner of his writing – e.g. the beautifully visualised dolmen in a barley field:

> The capstone,
> Set like a cauldron on three legs,
> Was marooned by the swimming crop.
> A gust, and the cromlech floated,
> Motionless at time's moorings . . .
>
> ('Ancient Monuments')

which is reminiscent of Van Gogh's paintings.

From 1945–9 he was a staff writer on *Picture Post* and since 1955 has been a documentary film maker with the B.B.C. In this position, which happily unites his artistic and literary interests, he has achieved international reputation. Especially distinguished are his films on Welsh poets: 'Under a Bright Heaven' (1966) on Vernon Watkins, 'A Bronze Mask' (1968) on Dylan Thomas, 'The Fragile Universe' (1969) on Alun Lewis, and 'R. S. Thomas, Priest and Poet' (1971).

In establishing himself as a gifted journalist he seems, for a time, to have lost confidence in his poetic inspiration: after the publication of *Indications* he decided, partly under the influence of Vernon Watkins, to wait until he was thirty before collecting his poems. He wrote and destroyed some 150 poems between the ages of 25 and 29, and it was not until about 1965 that he again sought publication. In 1969 *Requiem and Celebration* was published by Christopher Davies, Llandybie, and won a Welsh Arts' Council prize; in 1973, *Definition of a Waterfall* was published by Oxford University Press.

One reason for his fallow period is undoubtedly the very high standard of craftsmanship which he sets himself. For example, 'Salmon' was completed in November 1969 only after four and a half years' work involving about thirty drafts and three hundred or so worksheets. This exemplifies Walford Davies's comment quoted in our Introduction about Welsh poets' 'responsibility towards form'.

His recovery of inspiration seems to be connected with a re-exploration of the village community of his childhood and youth, which can be seen in such poems as 'My Grandfather and his Apple-tree', with its memorable portrait of:

A wild and drinking farmboy sobered by love
Of a miller's daughter and a whitewashed cottage
Suddenly to pay rent for,

and 'The Key', which shows both his superbly exact description:

The feather, askew
In the lock, would spray black
Droplets of oil on the threshold
And dandruff of feather-barb,

and the selection of appropriate imagery for his quest for truth. There is certainly nostalgia in poems of this kind, but it is controlled by humour and realism, never self-indulgent. The style is calm, meditative and poised, reminiscent in its quietly conversational rhythms of that of Robert Frost.

In the absence of a clear religious faith, John Ormond searches urgently for significance in life and death. 'Salmon', his marvellously vivid portrayal of the fasting fish who 'ache towards the one world/ From which their secret/Sprang', comes as near as is perhaps possible to an answer:

138

Why does this fasting fish
So haunt me? Gautama, was it this
You saw from river-bank
At Uruvela? was this
Your glimpse
Of holy law?

At His Father's Grave

Here lies a shoemaker whose knife and hammer
Fell idle at the height of summer,
Who was not missed so much as when the rain
Of winter brought him back to mind again.

He was no preacher but his working text
Was *See all dry this winter and the next.*
Stand still. Remember his two hands, his laugh,
His craftsmanship. They are his epitaph.

My Grandfather and His Apple-tree

Life sometimes held such sweetness for him
As to engender guilt. From the night vein he'd come,
From working in water wrestling the coal,
Up the pit slant. Every morning hit him
Like a journey of trams between the eyes;
A wild and drinking farmboy sobered by love
Of a miller's daughter and a whitewashed cottage
Suddenly to pay rent for. So he'd left the farm
For dark under the fields six days a week
With mandrel and shovel and different stalls.
All light was beckoning. Soon his hands
Untangled a brown garden into neat greens.

There was an apple-tree he limed, made sturdy;
The fruit was sweet and crisp upon the tongue
Until it budded temptation in his mouth.
Now he had given up whistling on Sundays,
Attended prayer-meetings, added a concordance
To his wedding Bible and ten children
To the village population. He nudged the line,
Clean-pinafored and collared, glazed with soap,
Every seventh day of rest in Ebenezer;
Shaved on a Saturday night to escape the devil.

The sweetness of the apples worried him.
He took a branch of cooker from a neighbour
When he became a deacon, wanting
The best of both his worlds. Clay from the colliery
He thumbed about the bole one afternoon
Grafting the sour to sweetness, bound up
The bleeding white of junction with broad strips
Of working flannel-shirt and belly-bands
To join the two in union. For a time
After the wound healed the sweetness held,
The balance tilted towards an old delight.

But in the time that I remember him
(His wife had long since died, I never saw her)
The sour half took over. Every single apple
Grew – across twenty Augusts – bitter as wormwood.
He'd sit under the box-tree, his pink gums
(Between the white moustache and goatee beard)
Grinding thin slices that his jack-knife cut,
Sucking for sweetness vainly. It had gone,
Gone. I heard him mutter
Quiet Welsh oaths as he spat the gall-juice
Into the seeding onion-bed, watched him toss
The big core into the spreading nettles.

The Ambush

(after Giovanni Bellini's The Assassination of St Peter Martyr)

Ring of black trees, late winter afternoon.
How came this bishop here in the elaborate fish-scales
Of his gold surplice, weighed down, unable to run,
Unable to flee to anywhere in the precise
Enclosing landscape, across the fields to the town
Or into the formality of the far pink hills?
Into the ring of trees wade men with swords.

The mute vermilion sun burns on their blades,
Reveals the fine, explicit, complex branches
On the horizon, every black twig exact;
With its deep falling it levers the horizon up.
The bishop and his attendants drop to their knees.
A slow light snow begins its imprecision
In this particular copse. The saints incur their wounds.
White flowers spring from the ground.
Earlier, woodcutters worked upon this spot;
Now see the tree-stumps bleed
Onto the snow with vegetable compassion
As these martyrs fall and die to rebellious men
Who make the copse a thicket with their spears.

The bloody sun's struck down. The eastern moon comes up.
In the thin beginning snow the saints
Cry out. Dusk, the still afternoon
Surrounds their cries, stifles their blood's music,
Their praise of the unfinished God.

I am the bishop, I am the men with the swords.

Cathedral Builders

They climbed on sketchy ladders towards God,
With winch and pulley hoisted hewn rock into heaven,
Inhabited sky with hammers, defied gravity,
Deified stone, took up God's house to meet Him,

And came down to their suppers and small beer;
Every night slept, lay with their smelly wives,
Quarrelled and cuffed the children, lied,
Spat, sang, were happy or unhappy,

And every day took to the ladders again;
Impeded the rights of way of another summer's
Swallows, grew greyer, shakier, became less inclined
To fix a neighbour's roof on a fine evening,

Saw naves sprout arches, clerestories soar,
Cursed the loud fancy glaziers for their luck,
Somehow escaped the plague, got rheumatism,
Decided it was time to give it up,

To leave the spire to others; stood in the crowd
Well back from vestments at the consecration,
Envied the fat bishop his warm boots,
Cocked up a squint eye and said, 'I bloody did that.'

Salmon

The river sucks them home.
The lost past claims them.
    Beyond the headland
It gropes into the channel
Of the nameless sea.
    Offshore they submit
To the cast, to the taste of it.
It releases them from salt,
Their thousand miles in odyssey
For spawning. It rehearsed their return
    From the beginning; now
    It clenches them like a fist.

The echo of once being here
Possesses and inclines them.
   Caught in the embrace
Of nothing that is not now,
Riding in with the tide-race,
   Not by their will,
Not by any will they know,
They turn fast to the caress
Of their only course. Sea-hazards done,
They ache towards the one world
   From which their secret
   Sprang, perpetuate

More than themselves, the ritual
Claim of the river, pointed
   Towards rut, casting
Their passion out. Weeping philosopher,
They re-affirm the world,
   The stars by which they ran,
Now this precise place holds them
Again. They reach the churning wall
Of the brute waterfall that shed
Them young from its cauldron pool.
   A hundred times
   They lunge and strike

Against the hurdles of the rock;
Though hammering water
   Beats them back
Still their desire will not break.
They coil and whip and kick,
   Tensile for their truth's
Sake; give to the miracle
Of their treadmill leaping
The illusion of the natural.
The present in torrential flow
   Nurtures its own
   Long undertow:

They work it, strike and streak again,
Filaments in suspense.
    The lost past shoots them
Into flight out of their element,
In bright transilient sickle-blades
    Of light; until upon
The instant's height of their inheritance
They chance in descant over the loud
Diapasons of flood, jack out of reach
And snatch of clawing water,
    Stretch and soar
    Into easy rapids

Beyond, into half-haven, jounce over
Shelves upstream; and know no question
    But, pressed by their cold blood,
Glance through the known maze.
They unravel the thread to source
    To die at their ancestry's
Last knot, knowing no question.
They meet under hazel trees
Are chosen and so mate. In shallows as
The stream slides clear, yet shirred
    With broken surface where
    Stones trap the creamy stars

Of air, she scoops at gravel with fine
Thrust of her exact, blind tail;
    At last her lust
Gapes in a gush on her stone nest
And his great squanderous peak
    Shudders his final hunger
On her milk; seed laid on seed
In spunk of liquid silk.
So in exhausted saraband their slack
Convulsions wind and wend galactic
    Seed in seed, a found
    World without end.

The circle's set, proportion
Stands complete, and
    Ready for death
Haggard they hang in aftermath
Abundance, ripe for the world's
    Rich night, the spear.
Why does this fasting fish
So haunt me? Gautama, was it this
You saw from river-bank
At Uruvela? Was this
    Your glimpse
    Of holy law?

The Key

Its teeth worked doubtfully
At the worn wards of the lock,
Argued half-heartedly
With the lock's fixed dotage.
Between them they deferred decision.
One would persist, the other
Not relent. That lock and key
Were old when Linus Yale
Himself was born. Theirs
Was an ageless argument.

The key was as long as my hand,
The ring of it the size
Of a girl's bangle. The bit
Was inches square. A grandiose key
Fit for a castle, yet our terraced
House was two rooms up, two down;
Flung there by sullen pit-owners
In a spasm of petulance discovering
That colliers could not live
On the bare Welsh mountain:

Like any other house in the domino
Row, except that our door
Was nearly always on the latch.
Most people just walked in, with
'Anybody home?' in greeting
To the kitchen. This room
Saw paths of generations cross;
This was the place to which we all came
Back to talk by the oven, on the white
Bench. This was the home patch.

And so, if we went out, we hid
The key – though the whole village
Knew where it was – under a stone
By the front door. We lifted up
The stone, deposited the key
Neatly into its own shape
In the damp earth. There, with liquid
Metal, we could have cast,
Using that master mould,
Another key, had we had need of it.

Sometimes we'd dip a sea-gull's
Feather in oil, corkscrew it
Far into the keyhole to ease
The acrimony there. The feather, askew
In the lock, would spray black
Droplets of oil on the threshold
And dandruff of feather-barb.
The deep armoreal stiffness, tensed
Against us, stayed. We'd put away
The oil, scrub down the front step.

The others have gone for the long
Night away. The evidence of grass
Re-growing insists on it. This time
I come back to dispose of what there is.
The knack's still with me. I plunge home
The key's great stem, insinuate
Something that was myself between
The two old litigants. The key
Engages and the bolt gives to me
Some walls enclosing furniture.

Ancient Monuments

They bide their time off serpentine
Green lanes, in fields, with railings
Round them and black cows; tall, pocked
And pitted stones, grey, ochre-patched
With moss, lodgings for lost spirits.

Sometimes you have to ask their
Whereabouts. A bent figure, in a hamlet
Of three houses and a barn, will point
Towards the moor. You find them there,
Aloof lean markers, erect in mud.

Long Meg, Five Kings, Nine Maidens,
Twelve Apostles: with such familiar names
We make them part of ordinary lives.
On callow pasture-land
The Shearers and The Hurlers stand.

Sometimes they keep their privacy
In public places; nameless slender slabs
Disguised as gate-posts in a hedge; and some,
For centuries on duty as scratching-posts,
Are screened by ponies on blank uplands.

Search out the farthest ones, slog on
Through bog, bracken, bramble: arrive
At short granite footings in a plan
Vaguely elliptical, alignments sunk
In turf strewn with sheep's droppings;

And wonder whether it was this shrunk
Place the guide-book meant or whether,
Over the next ridge, the real chamber,
Accurate by the stars, begins its secret
At once to those who find it.

Turn and look back. You'll see horizons
Much like the ones that they saw,
The tomb-builders, milleniums ago:
The channel scutched by rain, the same old
Sediment of dusk, winter returning.

Dolerite, gabbro, porphyry, fired
At the earth's young heart: how those men
Handled them. Set on back-breaking
Geometry, the symmetries of solstice,
What they awaited we, too, still await.

Looking for something else, I came once
To a cromlech in a field of barley.
Whoever farmed that field had true
Priorities. He sowed good grain
To the tomb's doorstep. No path

Led to the ancient death. The capstone,
Set like a cauldron on three legs,
Was marooned by the swimming crop.
A gust, and the cromlech floated,
Motionless at time's moorings.

Hissing dry sibilance, chafing
Loquacious thrust of seed
This way and that, in time and out
Of it, would have capsized
The tomb. It stayed becalmed.

The bearded foam, rummaged
By wind from the westerly sea-track,
Broke short, not over it. Skirted
By squalls of that year's harvest,
That tomb belonged in that field.

The racing barley, erratically bleached
Bronze, cross-hatched with gold
And yellow, did not stop short its tide
In deference. It was the barley's
World. Some monuments move.

Tricephalos

The first face spoke: Under sheep-run
And mole-mound and stifling glade,
I was awake though trapped in the mask

Of dirt. Counting the centuries,
I scrutinised the void, but its question
Stared me out. What was it I remembered

As, above me in the world, generation
Upon futile generation of tall trees,
Forest after forest, grew and fell?

It was that once the ease, the lease
Of a true spring saw my brow decked
With sprigs, my gaze complete and sensual.

My eyes (the second said) were fixed
In hunger for the whole regard
Of what might be, the god beyond the god.

Time and again the black loam blazed
And shuddered with false auguries.
Passionless, vigilant, I kept faith,

Invented systems, sounds, philosophies
In which some lean and listened-for,
Long-perfect melody might thrive.

The imagined dropped away, the perfect
Knew no advent. My sight was lost in sleep
And that stone sleep was haunted.

Two living garlands (spoke the third)
Strive to be one within our common skull.
They half-entwine the unavailing dreams

Fashioned from light that is, and words
That seem ours for the saying.
I await wisdom wise enough to know

It will not come. The inaccessible song
Upon whose resolution we, awake, expectant,
Yearning for order, lie, is the one tune

That we were born for. Its cadence
Shapes our vision and our blindness.
The unaccountable is my stone smile.

Dannie Abse

Dannie Abse was born in Cardiff on 22 September 1923 and educated at St Illtyd's College, Cardiff, before beginning his medical studies at the Welsh National School of Medicine. He began to write poetry while still at school, just before the Second World War, and his development was influenced by his brothers Wilfred and Leo (M.P. for Pontypool). He served in the R.A.F. Later he qualified as a medical practitioner at Westminster Hospital in London. While he was still a student there, Hutchinson published his first volume of poems, *After Every Green Thing* (1949). Subsequently the same publisher has brought out the following further volumes of his work: *Walking Under Water* (1952), *Tenants of the House* (1957), *Poems Golders Green* (1962), *A Small Desperation* (1968), *Selected Poems* (1970) and *Funland and other poems* (1973). In 1960 he won the C. H. Foyle Award.

Dr Abse is married and has a son and three daughters. Though he has spent most of his working life in London and still has a part-time job in a London chest clinic, he now manages to spend much of his time in his house at Ogmore-by-Sea, Glamorgan. In the academic year 1973–4 he was in the U.S.A. as writer-in-residence at Princeton University. His latest book, published by Hutchinson in 1974, is an autobiography entitled *A Poet in the Family*, a sequel to his famous autobiographical novel *Ash on a Young Man's Sleeve* (1954).

His childhood and young manhood in Wales are very important to Dr Abse, but he is a man of the world, with rich and varied experiences to call upon. 'The French Master' evokes memories of school, 'The Game' of the football match at Ninian Park, and other poems such as 'Return to Cardiff' and 'Car journeys: 1' show the importance of early personal and family experience. 'Pathology of Colours', on the other hand, is drawn from professional experience, and many poems such as 'A Night Out' and 'Moon Object' deal with broader moral, social and political matters.

As a young poet, Dannie Abse was exuberant with words,

influenced by Dylan Thomas, for whom he expresses admiration in 'Elegy for Dylan Thomas' not only in what he says but also by saying it in a form and style reminiscent of Thomas:

> Stranger, he is laid to rest
> not in the nightingale dark nor in the canary light.

'Epithalamion', a joyful, exuberant and witty poem, shows delight in what words can be made to perform:

> Singing, today I married my white girl
> beautiful in a barley field.
> Green on thy finger a grass blade curled,
> so with this ring I thee wed, I thee wed.

Many of the poems are directly personal, but the poet shows detachment and honesty:

> my first cigarette
> in the back lane, and, fool, my first botched love affair.
> First everything. Faded torments; self-indulgent pity.
>
> ('Return to Cardiff')

The sardonic tone of this is reminiscent of Philip Larkin's in 'I Remember, I Remember'. In later poems the style becomes much less rhetorical, more controlled and colloquial:

> Friends recommended the new Polish film
> at the Academy in Oxford Street.
> So we joined the ever melancholy queue
> of cinemas.
>
> ('A Night Out')

From the first, Dannie Abse showed a sense of humour and this, as his poetry develops, becomes subtle and penetrating:

> We asked the au pair girl from Germany
> if anyone had phoned at all, or called,
> and, of course, if the children had woken.
>
> ('A Night Out')

Throughout his work the poet has retained the ability to seize the attention of the reader and to engage his emotions in significant experience:

> So in the simple blessing of a rainbow,
> in the bevelled edge of a sunlit mirror,
> I have seen, visible, Death's artifact
> like a soldier's ribbon on a tunic tacked.
>
> ('Pathology of Colours')

Epithalamion

Singing, today I married my white girl
beautiful in a barley field.
Green on thy finger a grass blade curled,
so with this ring I thee wed, I thee wed,
and send our love to the loveless world
of all the living and all the dead.

Now, no more than vulnerable human,
we, more than one, less than two,
are nearly ourselves in a barley field –
and only love is the rent that's due
though the bailiffs of time return anew
to all the living but not the dead.

Shipwrecked, the sun sinks down harbours
of a sky, unloads its liquid cargoes
of marigolds, and I and my white girl
lie still in the barley – who else wishes
to speak, what more can be said
by all the living against all the dead?

Come then all you wedding guests:
green ghost of trees, gold of barley,
you blackbird priests in the field,
you wind that shakes the pansy head
fluttering on a stalk like a butterfly;
come the living and come the dead.

Listen flowers, birds, winds, worlds,
tell all today that I married
more than a white girl in the barley –
for today I took to my human bed
flower and bird and wind and world,
and all the living and all the dead.

The Game

Follow the crowds to where the turnstiles click.
The terraces fill. *Hoompa*, blares the brassy band.
Saturday afternoon has come to Ninian Park
and, beyond the goalposts, in the Canton Stand
between black spaces, a hundred matches spark.

Waiting, we recall records, legendary scores:
Fred Keenor, Hardy, in a royal blue shirt.
The very names, sad as the old songs, open doors
before our time where someone else was hurt.
Now, like an injured beast, the great crowd roars.

The coin is spun. Here all is simplified
and we are partisan who cheer the Good,
hiss at passing Evil. Was Lucifer offside?
A wing falls down when cherubs howl for blood.
Demons have agents: the Referee is bribed.

The white ball smacked the crossbar. Satan rose
higher than the others in the smoked brown gloom
to sink on grass in a ballet dancer's pose.
Again, it seems, we hear a familiar tune
not quite identifiable. A distant whistle blows.

Memory of faded games, the discarded years;
talk of Aston Villa, Orient, and the Swans.
Half-time, the band played the same military airs
as when The Bluebirds once were champions.
Round touchlines the same cripples in their chairs.

Mephistopheles had his joke. The honest team
dribbles ineffectively, no one can be blamed.
Infernal backs tackle, inside forwards scheme,
and if they foul us need we be ashamed?
Heads up! Oh for a Ted Drake, a Dixie Dean.

'Saved' or else, discontents, we are transferred
long decades back, like Faust must pay that fee.
The Night is early. Great phantoms in us stir
as coloured jerseys hover, move diagonally
on the damp turf, and our eidetic visions blur.

God sign our souls! Because the obscure staff
of Hell rule this world, jugular fans guessed
the result halfway through the second half,
and those who know the score just seem depressed.
Small boys swarm the field for an autograph.

Silent the stadium. The crowd have all filed out.
Only the pigeons beneath the roofs remain.
The clean programmes are trampled underfoot,
and natural the dark, appropriate the rain,
whilst, under lamp-posts, threatening newsboys shout.

Elegy for Dylan Thomas

    All down the valleys they are talking
  and in the community of the smoke-laden town.
Tomorrow, through bird-trailed skies, across labouring waves,
wrong-again Emily will come to the dandelion yard
    and, with rum tourists, inspect his grave.

    Death was his voluntary marriage,
and his poor silence sold to that rich and famous bride.
    Beleaguered in that essential kiss he rode
the whiskey-meadows of her breath till, mortal, voiceless,
    he gave up his nailed ghost and he died.

    No more to celebrate
his disinherited innocence or your half-buried heart
    drunk as a butterfly, or sober as black.
Now, one second from earth, not even for the sake
    of love can his true energy come back.

    So cease your talking.
Too familiar you blaspheme his name and collected legends:
    some tears fall soundlessly and aren't the same
    as those that drop with obituary explosions.
    Suddenly, others who sing seem older and lame.

But far from the blind country of prose,
wherever his burst voice goes about you or through you,
look up in surprise, in a hurt public house
or in a rain-blown street, and see how
no fat ghost but a quotation cries.

Stranger, he is laid to rest
not in the nightingale dark nor in the canary light.
At the dear last, the yolk broke in his head,
blood of his soul's egg in a splash of bright
voices and now he is dead.

The French Master

Everyone in Class II at the Grammar School
had heard of Walter Bird, known as Wazo.
They said he'd behead each dullard and fool
or, instead, carve off a tail for the fun.

Wazo's cane buzzed like a bee in the air.
Quietly, quietly, in the desks of Form III
sneaky Wazo tweaked our ears and our hair.
Walter Wazo, public enemy No. 1.

Five feet tall, he married sweet Doreen Wall,
and combmarks furrowed his vaselined hair;
his hands still fluttered ridiculously small,
his eyes the colour of a poison bottle.

Who'd think he'd falter, poor love-sick Walter
as bored he read out *Lettres de mon Moulin*;
his mouth had begun to soften and alter,
and Class IV ribbed him as only boys can.

Perhaps through kissing his wife to a moan
had alone changed the shape of his lips,
till the habit of her mouth became his own:
no more Walter Wazo, enemy No. 1.

'Boy,' he'd whine, 'yes, please decline the verb to have,'
in tones dulcet and mild as a girl.
'Sorry sir, can't sir, must go to the lav,'
whilst Wazo stared out of this world.

Till one day in May Wazo buzzed like a bee
and stung, twice, many a warm, inky hand;
he stormed through the form, a catastrophe,
returned to this world, No. 1.

Alas, alas, to the Vth Form's disgrace
nobody could quote Villon to that villain.
Again the nasty old mouth zipped on his face,
and not a weak-bladdered boy in the class.

Was Doreen being kissed by a Mr Anon?
Years later, I purred, 'Your dear wife Mr Bird?' –
Teeth bared, how he *glared* before stamping on;
and suddenly I felt sorry for the bastard.

Chalk

Chalk, calcium carbonate, should mean school –
a small, neutral stick neither cool nor hot,
its smell should evoke wooden desks slamming
when, squeaking over blackboards, it could not
decently teach us more than one plus one.

Now, no less pedagogic in ruder districts,
on iron railway bridges, where urchins fight,
an urgent scrawl names our failure – BAN THE BOMB,
or, more peculiarly, KEEP BRITAIN WHITE.
Chalk, it seems, has some bleeding purposes.

In the night, secretly, they must have come,
strict, clenched men in the street, anonymous,
past closed shops and the sound of running feet
till upstairs, next morning, vacant in a bus,
we observe a once blank wall assaulted.

There's not enough chalk in the wronged world
to spell out one plus one, the perfect lies.
HANDS OFF GUATEMALA – though slogans change,
never the chalk scraping on the pitched noise
of a nerve in violence or in longing.

As I Was Saying

Yes, madam, as a poet I *do* take myself seriously,
and, since I have a young, questioning family, I suppose
I should know something about English wild flowers:
the shape of their leaves, when this and that one grows,
how old mythologies attribute strange powers
to this or that one. Urban, I should mug up anew
the pleasant names: Butterbur, Ling, and Lady's Smock,
Jack-by-the-Hedge, Cuckoo-Pint, and Feverfew,
even the Stinking Hellebore – all in that W. H. Smith book
I could bring home for myself (inscribed to my daughter)
to swot, to know which is this and which that one,
what honours the high cornfield, what the low water,
under the slow-pacing clouds and occasional sun
of England.
    But no! Done for in the ignorant suburb,
I'll drink Scotch, neurotically stare through glass
at the rainy lawn, at green stuff, nameless birds,
and let my daughter, madam, go to nature class.
I'll not compete with those nature poets you advance,
some in country dialect, and some in dialogue
with the country – few as calm as their words:
Wordsworth, Barnes, sad John Clare who ate grass.

Return to Cardiff

'Hometown'; well, most admit an affection for a city;
grey, tangled streets I cycled on to school, my first cigarette
in the back lane, and fool, my first botched love affair.
First everything. Faded torments; self-indulgent pity.

The journey to Cardiff seemed less a return than a raid
on mislaid identities. Of course the whole locus smaller:
the mile-wide Taff now a stream, the castle not as in some black
gothic dream, but a decent sprawl, a joker's toy façade.

Unfocused voices in the wind, associations, clues,
odds and ends, fringes caught, as when, after the doctor quit,
a door opened and I glimpsed the white, enormous face
of my grandfather, suddenly aghast with certain news.

Unable to define anything I can hardly speak,
and still I love the place for what I wanted it to be
as much as for what it unashamedly is
now for me, a city of strangers, alien and bleak.

Unable to communicate I'm easily betrayed,
uneasily diverted by mere sense reflections
like those anchored waterscapes that wander, alter, in the Taff,
hour by hour, as light slants down a different shade.

Illusory, too, that lost, dark playground after rain,
the noise of trams, gunshots in what they once called Tiger Bay.
Only real this smell of ripe, damp earth when the sun comes out,
a mixture of pungencies, half exquisite and half plain.

No sooner than I'd arrived the other Cardiff had gone,
smoke in memory, these but tinned resemblances,
where the boy I was not and the man I am not
met, hesitated, left double footsteps, then walked on.

Pathology of Colours

I know the colour rose, and it is lovely,
but not when it ripens in a tumour;
and healing greens, leaves and grass, so springlike,
in limbs that fester are not springlike.

I have seen red-blue tinged with hirsute mauve
in the plum-skin face of a suicide.
I have seen white, china white almost, stare
from behind the smashed windscreen of a car.

And the criminal, multi-coloured flash
of an H-bomb is no more beautiful
than an autopsy when the belly's opened –
to show cathedral windows never opened.

So in the simple blessing of a rainbow,
in the bevelled edge of a sunlit mirror,
I have seen, visible, Death's artifact
like a soldier's ribbon on a tunic tacked.

Car Journeys: 1. Down the M4

Me! dutiful son going back to South Wales, this time afraid
to hear my mother's news. Too often, now, her friends are disrobed,
and my aunts and uncles, too, go into the hole, one by one.
The beautiful face of my mother is in its ninth decade.

Each visit she tells me the monotonous story of clocks.
'Oh dear,' I say, or 'how funny,' till I feel my hair turning grey
for I've heard that perishable one two hundred times before –
like the rugby 'amateurs' with golden sovereigns in their socks.

Then the Tawe ran fluent and trout-coloured over stones stonier,
more genuine; then Annabella, my mother's mother, spoke Welsh
with such an accent the village said, 'Tell the truth, *fach*,
you're no Jewess. *They're* from the Bible. *You're* from Patagonia!'

I'm driving down the M4 again under bridges that leap
over me then shrink in my side mirror. Ystalyfera is farther
than smoke and God further than all distance known. I whistle
no hymn but an old Yiddish tune my mother knows. It won't keep.

A Night Out

Friends recommended the new Polish film
at the Academy in Oxford Street.
So we joined the ever melancholy queue
of cinemas. A wind blew faint suggestions
of rain towards us, and an accordion.
Later, uneasy, in the velvet dark
we peered through the cut-out, oblong window
at the spotlit drama of our nightmares:
images of Auschwitz almost authentic,
the human obscenity in close-up.
Certainly we could imagine the stench.

Resenting it, we forgot the barbed wire
was but a prop, and could not scratch an eye:
those striped victims merely actors, like us.
We saw the Camp orchestra assembled,
we heard the solemn gaiety of Bach,
scored by the loud arrival of an engine,
its impotent cry, and its guttural trucks.
We watched, as we munched milk chocolate,
trustful children, no older than our own,
strolling into the chambers without fuss,
whilst smoke, black and curly, oozed from chimneys.

Afterwards, at a loss, we sipped coffee
in a bored espresso bar nearby
saying very little. You took off one glove.
Then to the comfortable suburb swiftly
where, arriving home, we garaged the car.
We asked the au pair girl from Germany
if anyone had phoned at all, or called,
and, of course, if the children had woken.
Reassured, together we climbed the stairs,
undressed together, and naked together,
in the dark, in the marital bed, made love.

Moon Object

After the astronaut's intrusion of moonlight, after
the metal flag, the computer-speeches – this little booty.

Is it really from the moon? Identify it if you can.
Test it, blue-eyed scientist, between finger and thumb.

Through a rainy city a car continues numb.
Its radio blanks out beneath a bridge.

In a restaurant, your colleague with a cold
is trying to taste his own saliva.

On the school piano, your wife's index finger
sinks the highest note. She hears the sound of felt.

Blue eyes, let your own finger and your thumb
slip and slide about it devilishly.

Don't you feel the gravity of the moon?
Say a prayer for the dead and murmur a vow.

Change your white coat for a purple cloak
and cage yourself a peacock or a gnat.

No, rational, you sniff it. But some holes in your front-brain
have been scooped out. A moon-howling dog would know.

Blue eyes, observe it again. See its dull appearance
and be careful: it could be cursed, it could be sleeping.

Awake, it might change colour like a lampshade
turned on, seething – suddenly moon-plugged.

Scientist, something rum has happened to you.
Your right and left eyes have been switched around.

Back home, if you dialled your own number now,
a shameless voice would reply, 'Who? Who?'

Three Street Musicians

Three street musicians in mourning overcoats
worn too long, shake money boxes this morning,
then, afterwards, play their suicide notes.

The violinist in chic, black spectacles, blind,
the stout tenor with a fake Napoleon stance,
and the loony flautist following behind,

they try to importune us, the busy living,
who hear melodic snatches of music hall
above unceasing waterfalls of traffic.

Yet if anything can summon back the dead
it is the old-time sound, old obstinate tunes,
such as they achingly render and suspend:

'The Minstrel Boy', 'Roses of Picardy'.
No wonder cemeteries are full of silences
and stones keep down the dead that they defend.

Stones too light! Airs irresistible!
Even a dog listens, one paw raised, while the stout,
loud man amazes with nostalgic notes – though half boozed

and half clapped out. And, as breadcrumbs thrown
on the ground charm sparrows down from nowhere,
now, suddenly, there are too many ghosts about.

Raymond Garlick

Of wholly English family (a Roman Catholic martyr named Nicholas Garlick was hanged, drawn and quartered on Derby Bridge in 1588), Raymond Garlick was born in London in 1926. But during the first decades of the century various members of his family settled at Deganwy, on the estuary of the Conway, so that in childhood Wales became for him the August country of holidays, of sand and sea, space and freedom, of non-suburbia.

He left school when he was fifteen, and worked for a time in a factory near London. From this he was delivered in 1943 when he read the first year of a degree in Latin and the philosophy and history of religions at the University of Leeds, transferring in 1944 to University College, Bangor, where he graduated in 1948 in philosophy and English literature.

For the next twelve years he taught at various schools in Bangor, Pembroke Dock and Blaenau Ffestiniog. At Pembroke Dock in 1949 he was one of the founders of *Dock Leaves*, which he edited until 1960 – changing its name in 1957 to *The Anglo-Welsh Review*. From these early years as a writer date his friendships with Roland Mathias (who succeeded him as editor) and R. S. Thomas. At Blaenau he enjoyed for five years the friendship of the venerable novelist John Cowper Powys, who had also settled there. But with these exceptions, and though there were editorial contacts with such writers as T. S. Eliot, David Jones, Idris Davies, Dylan Thomas, the writers with whom for many years he had personal acquaintance were writers in the Welsh language.

At the end of 1960 he settled in the Netherlands, joining the staff of the International School at Eerde Castle in the forest of Ommen, Overijssel. During his seven years there he travelled widely in western Europe. He returned to live in Wales in 1967, and is now director of Welsh Studies at Trinity College, Carmarthen. He lives in Llansteffan and is married, with a son and a daughter.

In 1968 Gwasg Gomer, Llandysul, published his collected poems, *A Sense of Europe*, which included all he wished to preserve of some half-dozen earlier publications. A further volume of poems, *A Sense of Time*, was published by Gwasg Gomer in 1972. Both were awarded Welsh Arts Council Literature Prizes. Raymond Garlick contributed the article on Anglo-Welsh Literature in *The New Catholic Encyclopaedia* (The Catholic University of America, Washington D.C.), and his *Introduction to Anglo-Welsh Literature* was published in 1972.

His work demonstrates a powerful capacity to evoke the detail of a landscape:

> Along the long
> shore's filigree,
> a ruffle and spread
> of peacock sea . . .
>
> ('Notes for a Picture')

and the atmosphere of a particular place:

> each bush had eyes,
> unseen but felt,
> each crouching log
> a grey-black pelt.
>
> ('Winter Walk')

'Agincourt' is only one of many poems that show his awareness of the historical associations of his many Welsh rural scenes. While normally avoiding propaganda, his work is very positively committed:

> These syllables swarm
> in Wales, Europe. Europe and Wales
> commit them to a theme and form.
>
> ('Personal Statement').

A meticulous craftsman who has never used 'free' verse, he always works towards appropriate form and utmost clarity and discrimination of statement:

> to pin
>
> a syntax on existence and to voice
> the vowels of being is the hot desire
> locked in my knotted limbs and body's vice.
>
> ('Biographical Note')

Shortage of space unfortunately prevents us from printing his recent interesting experiments such as 'Marwnad' and 'Documentary'.

Though his poetry is frequently personal, it is seldom ('A Touch of White' is an exception) narrowly so: 'Biographical Note' and 'Personal Statement' are concerned more with the poetry than with the poet. Whereas Yeats had to invent an esoteric historico-philosophical apparatus to underpin his poetry, Raymond Garlick has, with complete confidence, found identity, purpose and inspiration in Wales.

Dylan Thomas at Tenby

Into the pause, while peppermints were passed
after the strong piano's breathless Brahms,
he walked and took his place, sat down and cast

(expressionless of face) an eye abroad,
moving the carafe with a marked distaste.
His fame proclaimed, he looked politely bored

and crossed his legs and lit a cigarette,
screwing his eyes up at the smart of smoke.
So all was done and said. The scene was set

for speech, and nervously he stirred and spoke –
shuffling the pack of papers on his knee,
at random drew one, stared at it and woke

into awareness. Now the sleeping town
under the wood of Wales sat up and sang,
rose from its river bed and eiderdown

of ducks, strode heron-stilted through the dark
and rode white horses, nightmares from the sea,
across a *cantref* to this bay's bright arc

and the Noah of a poet calling there
to his creatures to come. Two by two, word
by word they marched from his mouth, pair by pair

to the beat of the drum of his tongue
and the trumpet of his lips. In the ships
of his speech the saga sailed and was sung.

And Tenby, their harbour, attended.
It was October, the month of birthdays.
The saga was nearly ended.

Biographical Note

And who am I? you ask. My mask is spare.
I live in a rakish body framed
about a spine like a buckled spire

or twisted spring, my uncurled crown of thorn.
One crystal tear of God, one devil's flame,
lies clear or leaps on this lop-sided throne.

As earth desires the rain, the womb the seed, pain
rest, conception birth, the burning lover
his beloved's breast: just so, to pin

a syntax on existence and to voice
the vowels of being is the hot desire
locked in my knotted limbs and body's vice.

And thus I am, and thus you see me now:
a hustings for a heart wrapped in a wrack,
lusting for words to shape itself anew.

Notes for a Picture

Look at Harlech
from above –
a landscape for
the turtle dove:

still as sunlight,
green as peace,
down which the eye
may fly at ease.

The *morfa*, now,
more caravanned
than all Arabia's
silver sand –

ten times better
than pink faced bands
of villas raw
as a butcher's hands.

Along the long
shore's filigree,
a ruffle and spread
of peacock sea –

too far, up here,
to read the runes
of litter on
the riddled dunes.

Gothic Eryri's
aquatint
and Wyddfa clear-lined
as a print

hang on the sky,
remote as art,
while tourists tear
their names apart.

And rising foursquare
over all,
geometry of tower
and wall:

the castle,
grey and verdigris –
articulation
now of peace;

a theorem
of human power
disproved by
swaying fern and flower.

Harlech teaches
that all things pass
but sea and mountain,
sand and grass.

Winter Walk

The squealing snow
beneath my tread
perhaps woke the lurking
words in my head:

'Sometimes, after weeks
of implacable snow,
one has been seen.
Better not go

too deep in the forest
in such a year:
hunger will run them
across the frontier.'

On the snow's white page
the textbook signs
slunk down the dazzle
between the pines –

the narrow inscription
of single dints,
each pad placed
in the other's prints,

a couple of hand-lengths
between each set.
The noiseless forest
spread out its net

of chiaroscuro –
like hyacinth
beneath the branches;
a labyrinth

of light on the paths,
a polar fur,
vividly slashing
the blue shade's blur.

Returning homewards,
threading the hours
and kilometres
back to the house,

each bush had eyes,
unseen but felt,
each crouching log
a grey-black pelt.

Consider Kyffin

Consider Kyffin, now – as Welsh
a word-spinner as you could wish,
who wove in both tongues, using yours
before you some four hundred years;
John Davies out of Hereford,
Holland of Denbigh – men who fired
their flintlocks through the border wall
loaded with English words as well.
Remember Lloyds and Llwyds, Vaughans,
who opened with their quills both veins
of language, giving life to myth –
the forked tongue in the dragon's mouth.
The others, too, who went astray
down some bypath of history –
their Welsh but not their Welshness lost:
in all, upon the muse's list
a hundred names – your pedigree,
you greener branches of the tree.

In silted bays of old bookshops –
shelved and becalmed like ancient ships
in saffron havens, I have rocked
their boats, long run aground and wrecked;
eased dusty covers open, looked,
clambered inside entranced, unlocked
each bulkhead page from stern to beak
and in the cabin of his book
come on the poet at his ease.
Some – seamen, scribbling in the haze
of voyages to where Wales joins
the world's end: Samwell, Poet Jones.
Others – upcountry parsons, squires,
hotblood students in Oxford squares,
curates penning the Poems of Hughes –
by candlelight in a creaking house
under the wheeling universe
cutting and polishing a verse.

They are the root from which you stem –
but you have never heard of them.

Fourth of May

Today, in this country
the size of Wales,
is remembrance day,
and the nightingales

articulate grief
in the waterlight
of the moon-soaked grass
as they did that night

when the frontier fields
were blurred with boots
and the moon was pitted
with parachutes.

For six of the twenty –
six years between,
I have imagined
the strange, unclean

sensation of living
in this place then.
On this still night
I think of the men

and women and children
crucified here,
the shock of blood
and the smell of fear

in the pink, scrubbed farms;
the school courtyard
an anvil hammered
by heels on guard;

the tall boots bruising
the sunlit lawn;
doom at the door
in the cold of dawn.

I think of this
and remember Wales,
the size of Holland.
Don't let the nails

of crucifixion
be hammered there –
employed by hands
half unaware.

Personal Statement

Mister to most, a formal man
(lives raised in splints grow stiff, no doubt,
training themselves to a handrailed plan

of plotted movements, fixed, foreseen),
for me a poem is first a frame.
Form is the cane on which I lean.

Round this beanpole tendril the lines
of communication, taut and green –
the vernal, sempiternal bines

of language reaching out to you;
the spread espaliers of speech
branching, budding, stretching through

from mere expression to the sky
and air of comprehension, where
every poem must open or die.

Change the image: communicate,
or else return to the writer. This
is also poetry's proper fate.

Sustain it: poetry must cram,
pack, concentrate, excise, exclude.
Art aspires to a telegram

of images. Each, like a flare
startling the unsuspecting dark,
must flood the no-man's landscapes where

the disparate identify
and incandescence focuses
a new relation, x is y.

Over the flux of being curves
the Very Light of metaphor,
probing truths in their knotted nerves;

under, the convoluted round
of the literal, the pock-marked earth,
the tongue's root and the eye's home-ground,

a here and now. These syllables swarm
in Wales, Europe. Europe and Wales
commit them to a theme and form.

And so you see the vivid braille
I seek to punch, and slide beneath
your fingertips: and why I fail.

Agincourt

Seven of the Welsh archers
whose arrows eclipsed the sun
in icy susurrations
when Agincourt was done
had gone there from Llansteffan.
When that day's death was won

if any of them lived
I wonder what they thought.
I live in Llansteffan
and I know Agincourt –
the bonemeal verdant meadows
over which they fought:

green places, both of them now,
but then, in 1415,
at Agincourt the blood
clotted the buttercups' sheen
and the earth was disembowelled
where stakes and hooves had been.

And far off, in Llansteffan,
castle, village and shore
flowered in the marigold sun.
Did those seven men explore
the contrast of this peace
with another English war?

A Touch of White

Six months we lived
on that precipice,
between the wall
and the abyss;
three of us trapped
upon the ledge
of being, on
the pit's sharp edge.
He was unmoved;
but sometimes we
glanced sideways down
at the swirling sea,
fathomless white,
of cloud below
and reeled in the rush
of vertigo –
reached out towards
the other's hand
and swayed there on
the heart's last strand.
White drift from
the sea we neared
touched forever
hair and beard.

Feet aslide on
the polished shale,
fingers clawing
the basalt wall,
I sought a sign.
It came like a knock
answered. We stood
on rock.

Bilingualism

Athwart the canal, green as Wales,
the great barge drifts. The tow-rope trails
slack in the water. On the bank
the barge-horse grazes, polished flank
turned to the water. Huge as an ark
the barge slides on: its tarred planks bark
the further shore, pointing away
to nowhere in the hot midday.
Browsing on, the indifferent horse
leaves the ark to its calm non-course
as time laps by.

        The problem's how
to turn the horse and the barge's prow
in one direction, harness each
to the other one before this reach
stills to a pool of green pondweeds
and, nose to stern across the reeds,
the barge lies like a monolith,
the stabled horse dies into myth,
means of communication silt
into a water-garden spilt
with dragon-flies, and marsh-worts sway
for picknickers on holiday.

Notes

Idris Davies (1905–53)

19   'I Was Born in Rhymney': this poem, completed in 1943, tells the story of Idris Davies' life. We have selected 34 of its 112 verses so as to cover the main events.

        Rhymney: town in Rhymney Valley, Monmouthshire.

        Apollo: Greek god of the sun and of poetry.

        Mammon: materialism (see Matthew vi, 24; Luke xvi, 13).

        Spurgeon: Charles Haddon Spurgeon (1834–92), famous Nonconformist preacher and author of sermons.

20   *MacDonald:* James Ramsay MacDonald (1866–1937), leader of the Labour Party and Labour Prime Minister in 1924 and 1929–31. Regarded by many socialists as a traitor for taking office as Prime Minister of the National (mainly Conservative) Government of 1931–5.

        Cook, Smith, Bevan: miners' leaders.

        Baldwin: Stanley Baldwin (1867–1947), Conservative Prime Minister 1923–4, 1924–9 and 1935–7. He defeated the General Strike (1926).

21   *city on the Trent:* Nottingham.

        D. H. Lawrence: (1885–1931), born Eastwood, near Nottingham. Like Idris Davies he was a critic of industrialism and its effect on ordinary people. This is what is meant by *savage Testament.*

        Yeats: William Butler Yeats (1865–1931). One of the greatest of twentieth-century poets. A powerful influence on Idris Davies (and on other Anglo-Welsh poets, e.g. Vernon Watkins; R. S. Thomas).

        Berkeley: George Berkeley (1685–1753), an anti-materialist philosopher.

178

and contrasts their suffering with the comfortable life of the rich.

'Tonypandy': a series of 6 poems describing the suffering of miners during their strike in 1926. The poem which we have included, number II, is, like 'Gwalia Deserta XII', in free verse.

'Saunders Lewis': (b. 1893) famous Welsh dramatist, writer and political activist, of international reputation.

Philistia: literally 'the land of the Philistines', here means England, which Idris Davies held responsible for the troubles, especially the industrial squalor, of Wales.

Vernon Watkins (1906–67)

32

'The Collier': may be compared and contrasted with the work of Idris Davies which it superficially resembles. The poet explores the experience and suffering of miners.

coloured coat; jealous; blood of a kid; pit; chain of gold; interpreted their dreams: see Genesis xxxvii and xli. Vernon Watkins compares the experience of the young miner to that of Joseph.

'Griefs of the Sea': expresses the continuous struggle between man and nature. Although the sea is shown as dangerous and destructive, it is a necessary and important part of God's creation – 'every drop is counted'. As in some poems of T. S. Eliot (whose work it resembles), there are lines of different lengths, but considerable use of rhyme.

35

'Returning to Goleufryn': Goleufryn, literally, means 'light hill', from *golau* and *bryn*. The poem evokes memories of childhood which are contrasted with the poet's adult experience. There is a memorable impression of Carmarthen.

They shall mount up like eagles: Isaiah xl, 31. The full quotation is 'But they that wait upon the Lord shall renew their strength: they shall mount up with wings as eagles.'

'The Feather': resembles 'Griefs of the Sea' and suggests that the sea must have living victims.

Furies: Greek goddesses of retribution.

'The Heron': contrasts the stillness of the heron with the movement and violence of the 'white horses of the sea'.

equinox: 21 March (here) and 23 September when night and day are equal. Believed to be times of high winds.

stallion and his mare: 'white horses' – waves.

'The Guest': shows the poet's detailed observation of nature.

Though dead, the owl still appears alive and dangerous.

fritillary light: fritillary is a name given to a species of lily and a type of butterfly. Both bear a chequered pattern.

'A Prayer': resembles 'A Prayer for my Daughter' by W. B. Yeats.

42

'Wordsworth': William Wordsworth (1770–1850), the most famous of the first generation of 'Romantic' poets, died on 23 April.

'The Red Lady': Vernon Watkins lived on and wrote about the Gower peninsula, an area famous for prehistoric remains as well as natural beauty. Paviland Cave was excavated by Dr Buckland in the nineteenth century. He found the skeleton of a Cro-Magnon man, buried with personal ornaments and an elephant's head, under a covering of red ochre (probably believed to have life-giving power because of its blood-like colour) and mistakenly identified it as that of a woman.

pollen's god: one way of discovering more about ancient burials is to examine and identify grains of pollen found under the burial. This shows what plants grew in the area at the time.

moon's Red Lady: the legend lives on.

'Strictness of Speech': the poet rejects empty words in favour of human contact and Christian love of one another.

peroration: the end of a speech; an oratorical performance.

R. S. Thomas (b. 1913)

'A Peasant': Iago Prytherch is a typical (archetypal) peasant (cf. Dai, Idris Davies's typical miner). He is unintelligent and smelly, but men like him keep the race alive.

'Cynddylan on a Tractor': R. S. Thomas tends to disapprove of machinery and mechanical progress. Driving a tractor, Cynddylan, though joyful, frightens the animals and is deaf to the birdsong. Compare/contrast him with Iago Prytherch.

'Invasion on the Farm': contrasts the countryman, with his slow speech and thoughts, with the townee, who talks and thinks rapidly. Prytherch feels disturbed and vulnerable – R. S. Thomas may well have in mind what some Welshmen call 'the English invasion'.

'Welsh Landscape': sometimes, as in this poem, R. S. Thomas grows impatient about the narrow-minded inactivity of Welsh people.

sped arrows: he may be thinking of the archers supplied by

Wales to medieval armies (cf. Raymond Garlick's 'Agincourt', p. 174).

51   'A Blackbird Singing': the bird's song suggests past suffering.
notes' ore: an image from the chemistry laboratory or foundry.

52   'Iago Prytherch': *surgery:* see e.g. 'Soil' (p. 49), where the peasant is seen 'docking mangolds'.

54   'Ninetieth Birthday': cf. 'Death of a Peasant' (p. 48) and 'Invasion on the Farm' (p. 48).

55   'Here': one of R. S. Thomas's finest poems. Describes the Crucifixion from the viewpoint of Christ looking down from the Cross.

'Sorry': the poet feels that his parents did not prepare him fully for adult life, but also reproaches himself for his doubts.

56   'For Instance': cf. 'Anniversary' (p. 53), another view of marriage.

57   'A Welshman in St James' Park':
Bosworth blind: at the Battle of Bosworth (1485), Henry Tudor, later Henry VII, defeated Richard III. Henry's army contained many Welshmen. Since then many other Welshmen have left Wales, especially to live in London.
'Service': describes the difficulty of making real contact with his congregation.

58   'No': a macabre account of the 'disease' of being a poet and of the poet's death.
'Reservoirs': shows the poet's bitterness with the English who destroy Welsh life and culture (cf. 'Saunders Lewis' p. 30 and 'The Flooded Valley' p. 89), and with the Welsh for letting them do it (cf. 'Welsh Landscape' p. 50).

59   'Cain': see Genesis iv.
the doomed tree: the Cross where God (the Son) was crucified.

60   'The Island': cf. 'Service' (p. 57). Explores the problem of suffering in the world. Reminiscent of the Book of Job.
suppurate: gather, or ooze pus.

Dylan Thomas (1914–53)

63   'I Have Longed to Move Away': an early poem (written age 19). Shows the desire of a young man to get away from the place where he has grown up (Thomas went to London the next year), but is more concerned with the poet's inner feelings than with a mere wish for excitement and change.

might explode: the image is from fireworks. He is not sure whether, if he leaves, he may not lose something essential to his being.

Neither by night's ancient fear: this and the next three lines echo the style of W. H. Auden, an influential poet of the thirties.

64

'And Death Shall Have No Dominion': Thomas was, from an early stage in his writing, concerned with death. Here he suggests that death cannot defeat mankind because, after death, human beings live on as part of the eternal universe.

Stars at elbow and foot: like the hunter, Orion, who, after death became a constellation.

'The Hand That Signed the Paper': this also resembles the work of Auden (e.g. 'Epitaph on a Tyrant') and can also be compared with 'Strictness of Speech' (p. 43), though it is much more frightening and describes the heartlessness of powerful politicians, symbolised by the hand that signs, e.g. a declaration of war that leads to the death of many innocent people.

65

'Light Breaks Where No Sun Shines': a punning and ingenious poem in which man is seen, as in 'And Death Shall Have No Dominion', as part of the fabric of nature. Natural phenomena like tides, sunrise, wind, the moon are used to interpret human existence.

ghosts with glow-worms: the image is of deep-sea fish which generate their own light by means of phosphorescence.

File: a pun.

A candle: the penis, the male sex-organ.

poles: man compared to the Earth; man's North is his *skull*, his South his feet.

rod: an image from water-divining.

'This Bread I Break': first traces the bread back to the grain and the wine back to the grape, then unites them in Christ and the Communion Service where the bread represents the flesh and the wine the blood of the Saviour. Again man and Nature are used to interpret one another.

'Where Once the Waters of Your Face': he looks back, as so often, to lost childhood and its ecstasy. The waters are the tides of Swansea Bay and the poet contrasts the hope of childhood with the sense of death that developed as he grew older.

mermen: imagined by the child.

The green unraveller: Time.

clocking: suggests the sound of the water.

dolphined sea: cf. 'That dolphin-torn, that gong-tormented sea' in W. B. Yeats's 'Byzantium', another poem concerned with Time and Death.

'Once it was the Colour of Saying': describes the process of writing poetry, which came more easily to the young than to the older Dylan Thomas. He sees creation as a destructive act and it seems likely that the failure of his inspiration destroyed him eventually – as he suggests by 'my saying shall be my undoing' (also a pun, however). Cf. 'In My Craft or Sullen Art' (p. 72).

mitching (or miching): playing truant.

68 'The Hunchback in the Park': a beautiful evocation of boyhood experience in Cwmdonkin Park. A hunchback did frequent the park during the poet's boyhood.

garden lock: compares the opening of the park gates to the opening of lock gates. As water fills up the lock, so, the poet fancifully suggests, trees and water fill up the park.

Sunday sombre: as serious as Sunday.

loud zoo: the boys imagined wild animals.

69 *old dog:* continues the image from stanza 2.

bell time: a pun on 'bed time'.

a woman figure: the hunchback consoles himself by imagining a beautiful, perfect woman who will love him.

unmade: like an unmade bed.

'Poem in October': the poet, aged 30, describes Laugharne and the country around it and looks regretfully back to the happier days of his childhood. This poem and 'Fern Hill' are the supreme expression in Thomas's work of the exuberant delight of childhood seen with regret by the grown man. Cf. 'Returning to Goleufryn' (p. 35).

priested: the heron makes a sombre, priest-like figure.

70 *Over the border:* out of the town, but also out of his present life and back into an earlier one.

fond climates: the pleasant summer days of childhood.

twice told fields: a pun on 'twice told tales'.

71 'A Refusal to Mourn the Death, by Fire, of a Child in London': written March 1945. He will not mourn because, as he has suggested in 'And Death Shall Have No Dominion' (p. 64), the girl is not extinct but survives as part of the eternal universe. Notice the magnificent way in which the poem marches to a climax.

sea tumbling in harness: Cf. 'I sang in my chains like the sea' ('Fern Hill').

183

Zion . . . synagogue: all things declare the glory of God, so a drop of water or an ear of corn may be a place of worship.

sow my salt seed: salt was sowed to make land infertile (he probably intends a reference to human fertilisation also).

grave: a pun.

stations: a pun (on Stations of the Cross).

72 *friends . . . grains . . . mother:* in death everything is united, human beings and the natural world.

After the first death: physical death is insignificant in comparison with life eternal.

'In My Craft or Sullen Art': Written October 1945, this poem is another attempt to define the poet's purpose in writing. He suggests that poetry is written for its own sake, not for glory or profit, but for love. He describes creation as difficult (*sullen*) and strange (*moon rages*). (Cf. 'Once It Was the Colour of Saying' p. 67.)

common wages: love of what he is creating.

spindrift: the spray blown by wind from the crests of waves. It is light and, like pages, white. His poetry is fragile, may not survive. A typical natural image.

Alun Lewis (1915–44)

75 'Raiders' Dawn': the title poem of Alun Lewis's first volume of poems, published in 1942. Deals with the threat to civilisation and, more particularly, love and beauty.

Eternity's masters,/Slaves of Time: lovers' experience is timeless in intensity, but Time parts them.

'The Rhondda': Cf. poems by Idris Davies (e.g. 'The Angry Summer 10', p. 28).

76 *Circe:* in the *Odyssey* of Homer, the enchantress who lured Odysseus' companions to drink from the magic cup which turned them into swine. Alun Lewis compares industrialism to a whore luring men into the mines and making beasts of them.

'The Mountain over Aberdare':

scrutting: scratching at spoil heaps for pieces of coal.

77 *rune:* runes are an ancient form of writing that takes the form of lines and strokes. Runes are found on Celtic crosses, in and outside Wales. He means that the hills show the marks made on them by industrial activity over the years.

'The Defeated': a lament for the sufferings of the Welsh nation, though, like R. S. Thomas, the poet blames the Welsh as much as their conquerors for the situation in which he sees them.

Euphrates and Tigris: between these rivers lies Mesopotamia (now Iraq and Syria), the cradle of ancient civilisation, where the Sumerians lived from 3500 B.C. onwards. By comparison, Welsh civilisation is very young, but it is honoured by the comparison.

78   'All Day It Has Rained': resembles 'Rain' by Edward Thomas, a poet of the First World War with whom Lewis partly identified himself.

79   *Sheet and Steep:* Villages in Hampshire where Edward Thomas lived.

Shoulder o' Mutton: a hill near Steep.

till a bullet stopped his song: Thomas was killed near Arras in 1917, not by a bullet, but by the blast from a stray shell.

'Infantry': uses wartime images to interpret the soldiers' experience (*iron rations, black market*). Also uses religious imagery connected with the Crucifixion (*stations* suggests Stations of the Cross; *unction* the anointing of Christ's feet). Reminiscent of poems by Wilfred Owen (1893–1918).

like a girl: denied female company, soldiers ache for it as their bones ache with cold.

Rum: in the First World War rum was issued to troops before they went 'over the top'.

The poem is a sonnet, though the rhyme scheme – ABAB CDED FGFGFG – is unusual.

80   'A Welsh Night': *yellow hands:* lyddite, an explosive containing picric acid, stains the hands yellow.

shroud or shawl: suggests the balance in the poem between the sense of death (shroud) and that of life (shawl).

'The Peasants': are Indian. Lewis was posted to India in 1942 and the rest of the poems in this selection were written while he was there.

Creation touching: the women are pregnant (perhaps an echo of 'if the Sun breed maggots in a dead dog, being a God kissing carrion': *Hamlet*, 2, ii).

81   'Bivouac': describes the feelings of soldiers camped at night in the Indian countryside.

leathery vendetta: animals preying upon one another.

mantillas: a mantilla is a kind of veil. He seems to be referring to the fur of beasts of prey.

185

withering obsession: the experience leaves the soldiers with a profound sense of loneliness and isolation.

82 'The Crucifixion': note the conversational tone, which contrasts with the terrible subject. The style resembles that of 'All Day It Has Rained' (p. 78). Cf. subject with 'Here' (p. 55).

passively passionate: word-play on the two meanings of 'passive' – (a) letting things happen, (b) suffering; and 'passion' – (a) powerful feeling, (b) suffering. Christ cared deeply and suffered bitterly but with complete ('passive') acceptance.

other than he had imagined: reference to the Agony in the Garden when Christ asked God to let the cup pass from him.

convulsing his Father: God being 'three-in-one', the Father suffers the agony of the Son.

stigma: mark where the nails were driven in.

strained: Lewis is trying to give an accurate impression of the physical agony of hanging on the cross.

'The Mahratta Ghats': an extensive range of mountains.

83 *Siva* (or Shiva): third person of the Hindu Trinity, representing the destructive principle in life, but also reproductive or renovating power (hence *seed*). Siva means 'the blessed one'.

bumming: carrying.

'In Hospital: Poona (1)': there are two poems about the experience of being in hospital in Poona. Lewis spent 6 weeks there in 1943, first with a jaw broken playing football, then with dysentery. This poem is a moving expression of love for his wife and feeling for Wales.

84 'Song': a symbolic expression of feelings about leaving his wife to fight in the war. There is a fine juxtaposition of everyday detail and deep feeling, especially in the last two verses. The poem ends with a sense of death.

85 'Goodbye': about parting from his wife to go to India.

Time's chalice: the troubles that the future holds.

Roland Mathias (b. 1915)

89 'The Flooded Valley': the title poem of a volume published in 1960. A farmer laments the loss of his land for a reservoir (Cf. 'Reservoirs' p. 58).

not again to sell: there is no land on which to raise sheep.

Caerfanell: stream running past the house and into the reservoir.

gave me a fish for my stone: he threw a stone into the water and a fish rose.

Grwyney: the rivers Grwyne and Grwyne Fawr join near Crickhowell, Breconshire.

church of Patricio: 4½ miles north-east of Crickhowell is the church of Partrishow or Patrishow.

Senni: Breconshire river. Flows into the Usk at Sennybridge.

90

'Hawk': *goitred:* bulging neck of rock.

cut: gully.

Jehu-crack: whip-crack of thunder (after the Biblical 'furious driver').

perfunctory: sparse.

irate as a stone: angry-looking, but still.

squireen's cavil: a squireen is an unimportant squire; a cavil is a trifling objection. The hawk seems to be standing on its dignity like one easily offended.

nemesis: Greek goddess of retribution.

knuckle: show respect (as in 'knuckle under').

unshrives: blames, curses.

laverock: poetic word for the skylark.

91

'Argyle Street': a street in Pembroke Dock on Milford Haven, where the poet once lived.

in chancery: subject of legal action; in an awkward predicament.

tufted: plants are growing in the crevices.

'For Warren Davies': fine tribute to a man who moved from a farming family to be a shipwright.

viking-cast dropped out of conquest: he looks like the descendant of Vikings who raided Pembrokeshire and settled parts of it.

jawed like Magnus at the holocaust: Magnus was a tenth-century Norse king, responsible for many a massacre (holocaust). Davies looks like the picture of a Viking.

A crab for history: a fig for history!

South Hook: a headland near Milford Haven.

caulk: make watertight the seams between the planks of a ship.

bolt the herring-set: set nets for herrings.

Hakin Point: Hakin is part of Milford Haven (town).

92

Pater tackle: Pater is an old name for Pembroke Dock. Davies is happy in the place where he has settled.

spinnaker: type of sail.

pill: creek.

Lawrenny: village on the upper reaches of Milford Haven inlet.

plat: plot of ground.

Cleddau: the Western Cleddau flows through Haverfordwest and joins the Eastern Cleddau at the north end of Milford Haven. They flow on as the Daucleddau.

Jobbers: literally 'brokers'. He means people like himself, getting together for a chat and to put the world to rights.

casuists: arguers, with the suggestion that the arguments are not entirely fair.

93   *court in purple:* royalty, especially emperors, wear purple. The purple clematis 'ennobles' the place where it grows.

page: the newly growing plant pages (announces) the spring.

preening cast: the transplanted clematis flourishes.

recouple: Davies is dying and the poet wonders if in some way the new life of the plants could prolong his life.

unmanned: even the morning and the sun mourn this man.

'Freshwater West': an extensive bay in South Pembrokeshire, about 2 miles west of Castlemartin. Watching, or remembering, the waves break over the rocks and sand, the poet muses nostalgically about his younger days.

ad finitum: play on words – the usual expression, 'ad infinitum', means for ever. Ad finitum means 'for a limited time'.

94   *old-white/With frays:* the foam of the waves, turned off-white by the sand they have disturbed.

Broken like sand: the poet sees his body worn away by time as rocks are worn into sand by sea and wind.

'Searching Spring': is reminiscent, especially in style, of 'Spring' by Gerard Manley Hopkins (1844–89), the second line of which reads 'When weeds, in wheels, shoot long and lovely and lush'. The poet shows spring as a violent season.

our disaster and grave wound: like a human being who is fatally wounded; *grave wound* is a pun.

Province under boots: soil, with all its potential growth.

covenant: the poet feels he has to take care of himself.

'Craswall': place on the Hereford/Breconshire border.

stirrup: the shepherd is riding a pony.

95   *canting neck:* tilted rock (cf. *goitred neck* p. 90).

'For an Unmarked Grave': cf. 'Death of a Peasant' (p. 48). The man mourned is important only to the poet, whose uncle he was.

pallet: mattress; poor bed.

corpse him: bury him.

hard-tack joke: though dying, he can joke.

sputum: something spat out, suggesting the man died of tuberculosis.

Cwmcamlais: about 5 miles west of Brecon. The poet's uncle is buried in the chapel there.

loins were water: since he was in the womb.

Senni: land around the Senni river, Breconshire.

Hardening of Wales: Wales is ageing, dying (cf. arteries).

96   'Departure in Middle Age': the poet reviews younger days with regret (cf. 'Freshwater West' p. 93).

dazed as cock-crow: the half-awake feeling one has at dawn.

Fan: peak, mountain. Various peaks in the Black Mountains and Brecon Beacons are so called.

pinafore: as worn by a young child.

drop your pretences: a pun, meaning both 'rain' and 'clear away'.

'Freshwater West Revisited': cf. 'Freshwater West' (p. 93). H examines the savagery of sea and rocks.

ellipses of force: the movement of waves and wind.

socius: comrade; ally (Latin).

girds up: holds together – marram grass is often planted to prevent sand being blown away.

proffer a parody: make fun of. He compares the attack of the elements to the charge of a bull. Inland one feels safe.

97   'They Have Not Survived': a poem in memory of Welsh peasants and miners, who lived and died hard.

cenedl: type, nation.

tallut: hay-loft (Welsh *taflawd*).

rhos: moor.

swarming . . . queen: peasants compared to bees.

milgis: greyhounds.

98   'Some Tight-lipped Wave':

bedlam: madness.

polities: state of order (before the crash).

Kastellorizon: island, part of Dodekanesos, off southern coast of Turkey. The *sea of ancients* is the Mediterranean.

Minoan savageries: the Minoan civilisation flourished on Crete and elsewhere from about 3000 to 1200 B.C. Minos, king of Crete, made the Athenians supply seven men and seven maidens each year to feed the Minotaur, a monster which he kept in the Labyrinth, an underground maze. The poet compares his dead friends to the innocent sacrifices.

189

tight-lipped wave: eventually the dead couple will, in a sense, return to their seaside home when the tiny aftermath of the wave from their crash reaches these shores.

'A Letter from Gwyther Street': the poet revisits Pembrokeshire and some friends who live there. As in 'Freshwater West' and 'Freshwater West Revisited', he links the passing of time with the elements, especially the sea.

Barafundle: a beautiful bay in S. Pembrokeshire, about a mile south-east of Stackpole.

colloped: eaten into slices.

99   'New Lease': the poet is concerned about the depopulation of Wales and sees in the abandoned house the stimulus for a 'new lease of life' for Welshmen who care. He evokes memories of Celtic history, great times of the distant past.

captor country: some Welshmen feel that Wales is still in a sense 'occupied' by England.

Llifiau: character in *The Gododdin*, a poem by the late sixth-century Welsh poet Aneirin. He comes from beyond the frontier and is a Pict, not a Celt, but he shares the struggle.

Bannog: the northern frontier of the ancient Celtic lands, between Stirling and Oakhill, Scotland.

Picts: the 'painted people' of Scotland and Ireland. Hadrian's Wall was built to keep them out. After the Romans left, they raided far into the south.

Harri Webb (b. 1920)

103   'Synopsis of the Great Welsh Novel': one of the funniest of Anglo-Welsh poems. The poet imagines a novel made up of cliché situations from many novels about Wales.

Revival: a time of concentrated religious activity.

Elijah: oratorio by Handel.

Con Club: Conservative Club.

Free Wales Army: pseudo-military organisation of uncertain strength pledged to fight for the freedom of Wales.

National: the National Eisteddfod.

Sir Lewis Morris: (1833–1907) born Carmarthen, educated Queen Elizabeth Grammar School and Jesus College, Oxford. A rather poor poet whose *Works* were published in 1891.

104   'The Antennae of the Race': the title refers to poets, or writers and the poem, humorously, but with serious intent, warns that their perceptions get ignored by more practical people.

R.D.F.: Radar stands for 'Radio, Direction and Ranging'. In the early days it was known as 'Radio Direction Finder'.

rouged: inflamed; chapped.

collision mat: for covering a hole after a collision.

'Dyffryn Woods': evokes the poignant mixture of ugliness and beauty found in South Wales mining valleys. Cf. Idris Davies. The woods are in the Rhondda, near Mountain Ash, where the poet works.

Cynon/Our nameless poet: refers to an anonymous eighteenth-century Welsh poem entitled *Coed Glyn Cynon.*

answer back: the earth, subsiding into old mine-workings, distorts and sometimes destroys buildings.

lungs of stone: caused by pneumoconiosis, a miners' disease caused by breathing in a dusty atmosphere.

'Cywydd O Fawl': a *cywydd* (complex form of Welsh poetry in which masculine and feminine rhymes alternate) of praise.

yn null y gogogynfeirdd: in the style of the Gogynfeirdd (for fun he adds an extra *go*), Welsh poets of the twelfth to fourteenth centuries, noted for their complicated poems praising Welsh lords.

à gogo: (not Welsh) a joke showing that this is a 'pop' *cywydd.*

Shadrach: see Daniel iii, 12–28.

ach y fi: nasty! ugh!

Aberteifi: Cardigan.

Twp: stupid.

Arts Council: the Welsh Arts Council has been generous and effective in promoting literature in Wales.

Seiat: fellowship meeting.

Salem: typical name for a Welsh Nonconformist Chapel (cf. the short stories of Caradoc Evans, whose style is imitated here).

Beibil Moses his manna: manna given to Moses in the Bible.

107

'Cilmeri': in Breconshire, the place where Llywelyn, the last native Welsh prince, was killed in 1282. A huge stone commemorates him. The poet laments the increasing erosion of the Welsh way of life. He blames the Welsh people for this.

Aberffraw: small village in Anglesey, once a seat of government of the princes of North Wales.

Branwen: the *Mabinogion* tells of Branwen, a British princess who married an Irish king and was the cause of war between Britain and Ireland (the Celtic Helen of Troy). She died of a broken heart and was buried in a four-sided grave on the bank of the River Alaw, Anglesey. Such a grave was excavated there in 1813.

Segontium: Roman stronghold near Caernarvon. Caernarvon Castle (the *stone battleship*) was partly built with stones taken from Segontium (the *hall brought from Conway*).

David's Sapphire: part of the booty taken from David, brother of Llywelyn the Last, when he was captured by Edward I in 1283.

Croes Naid: Cross of Princes of Gwynedd, plundered by Edward I and put with the Crown Jewels.

Here is only stone: deliberate echo of 'Here is no water but only rock' (T. S. Eliot, 'The Waste Land' V, l. 331) used to strengthen the feeling of desolation.

In a dead season: echoes 'Thoughts of a dry brain in a dry season' (T. S. Eliot, 'Gerontion'), for the same purpose.

the slack dunes: used to suggest the desolation spreading over Wales, especially as the result of depopulation.

augural birds: the Romans believed that the future could be forecast from the flight of birds. An augurer forecasts the future.

108   'Israel': Welsh people are castigated because, unlike the Jews, they have not fought to keep their independence and culture.

sweat glands had atrophied: no longer did hard physical work.

lambs to the slaughter: e.g. in Nazi gas-chambers.

Maccabeus: struck the first blow for liberty during the persecution of the Jews under Antiochus IV.

deserts are green: The Green Desert is the title of a volume of Harri Webb's poems.

'In Memory of Harri Jones': T. Harri Jones (see pp. 124–36).

Irfon: river in Breconshire (where Harri Jones was born).

guilty water: Llywelyn the Last was killed near Irfon Bridge. Cilmeri is between the Irfon and the Chwefri, a river that joins it near Builth Wells.

Epynt: Mynydd Epynt, mountain near Llangammarch, Breconshire.

Dylife: abandoned mining area in Montgomeryshire.

Clywedog: tributary of the Severn; rises near Dylife.

Silurian: rocks of the Palaeozoic Era, named after the Silures, a tribe that lived in South Wales.

109   'The Stone Face': a fine poem in which the discovery of a stone carving which may represent Llywelyn ap Iorwerth (1187–1240), 'The Great', so called because he created a strong

Welsh feudal state and exercised overlordship over practically the whole of independent Wales, leads to the familiar exhortation to modern Welshmen to recapture their old greatness.

Deganwy: in Caernarvonshire. The ruins of an early Norman castle there are the site where the carving was found.

John: King of England, who married his daughter, Johanna, to Llywelyn ap Iorwerth.

his grandson: Llywelyn ap Gruffudd (1246–82), known as 'The Last'. Prince of Wales. His death at Cilmeri on 11 December 1282 ended all hope of an independent Welsh state.

Great Orme: a headland near Llandudno.

110   *cleansing of the eyes:* of the carved head, but also of the modern inheritors of Llywelyn's tradition.

Leslie Norris (b. 1921)

113   'An Evening by the Lake': walking in Cyfarthfa Park at Merthyr Tydfil, Leslie Norris remembers his childhood here and regrets the loss of youth. The passage about the boat-race resembles Wordsworth's 'Prelude' (Book I, l. 357 ff., and Book II, l. 55 ff.), another poem which is about youth and childhood.

115   'The Ballad of Billy Rose': cf. Dannie Abse's 'The Game' (p. 154).

resin: boxers step into a tray of resin dust to prevent them slipping on the canvas of the ring.

as bright as his name: a moving pun.

116   *three sharp coins:* the poet feels he has betrayed the memory of this great boxer by giving him charity.

'Gardening Gloves': about the skill in gardening which the poet has inherited from his father and his ancestors and which he seems to put on with the old gloves.

gargoyle: carved monster used as water spout on a church.

119   'Early Frost': *frostnails:* nails hammered into the hoofs of the ponies to help them get a grip on frosty roads.

in a cold fever for: very much looking forward to (a pun).

120   'Stones': *onyx:* white, yellow, black, brown or red agate.

chalcedony: a white or bluish white mineral.

jasper: opaque quartz.

quartzite: metamorphosed sandstone.

121   'A True Death': Vernon Watkins died in the U.S.A. in 1967.

charred hills: in the Swansea area.

He knew: Watkins lived on and wrote about the Gower peninsula.

122 *tormentil:* potentilla erecta, a small yellow wild-flower.

'Stone and Fern': the poet has been tempted to leave but has decided, though he feels doomed, to remain.

123 'Bridges': an accurate account and vivid picture of bridges, but suggests difficulties of communication (cf. 'Bilingualism' p. 176) and the excitement of exploration and progress.

images: the bridge-halves are reflected in the water.

slid: made slippery by the men working on them.

policies of inaction: cf. difficulty of communication.

Harri Jones (1921–65)

126 'The Pride of the Morning': resembles 'As I Walked Out One Evening' by W. H. Auden, a poet whom Harri Jones often echoes. He thinks of his over-confident youth when he believed, wrongly, that he was self-sufficient.

ambiguities: double or multiple meanings.

fallibility: a poet seldom knows exactly what he has said.

127 'It Is Not Fear': a villanelle, a form liked by Auden. The poet offers advice, suggesting that the worst sort of fear is that of a particular thing.

128 'A Promise to My Old Age': cf. 'The Pride of the Morning' p. 126.

cumber: obstruct.

129 *farrow:* give birth to.

'Adam's Song After Paradise': Adam speaks to Eve after they have been driven from Paradise for eating the fruit of the Tree of Knowledge of Good and Evil.

Torn from my side: according to Genesis, Eve was created from one of Adam's ribs.

furtively: sexual love was innocent before the Fall; after the Fall they became ashamed of it.

am content: Adam chose expulsion from Paradise and death rather than be parted from Eve.

130 'The Beast at the Door': title-poem of Harri Jones's third volume of poetry. An allegorical account of the dangerous, lustful side of the poet's (and human) nature.

big-pilled: with large testicles.

131 'Mr Jones as the Transported Poet': once criminals were

transported to Australia. The poet puns on the two meanings of the word.

'Back': in this poem, suitably dedicated to R. S. Thomas, the poet, while critical of Wales, shows his abiding love for it.

132   *shamed memories of Glyn Dwr*: Owain Glyn Dwr (1359?–1416?) led the Welsh rebellion against Henry IV.

Saunders Lewis's aerodrome: in 1936 Saunders Lewis, D. J. Williams and the Rev. Lewis Valentine set fire, as a gesture of protest, to some buildings at an R.A.F. airfield on the Llŷn Peninsula. They then gave themselves up to the police and were tried and imprisoned in Wormwood Scrubs.

'Girl Reading John Donne': Donne (1573–1631) is one of the great love poets. This poem tells of a lecturer who is attracted to one of his students and of how reading Donne stimulates her passion. While she burns with love, he marks assignments.

Goodmorrow: 'The Good-morrow', by Donne, tells of a man and woman in bed together and expresses the joy of physical passion. Here the poet echoes the line 'And now good morrow to our waking souls'.

133   *a great Prince*: from 'The Extasie' by Donne, where two lovers are holding hands. At the end of the poem it is suggested that they should make love because if they do not 'a great Prince in prison lies', i.e. they miss the extremely powerful experience of physical love.

ampersand: the sign &.

Elegie: Donne wrote 20 'elegies', a typical one being 'To His Mistress Going to Bed', one line of which reads 'O my America! my new-found-land'.

marking time: a pun.

canicule: heat.

134   'My Grandfather Going Blind': cf. 'My Grandfather and his Appletree' (p. 139).

cataracts: disease of the eye which makes the lens opaque.

135   'Welsh Childhood': *lacerated*: torn: the appearance of the pine needles and branches.

'Builth Wells': *Buallt*: Welsh form of Builth.

Wye: Builth stands on the River Wye.

John Ormond (b. 1923)

139   'My Grandfather and his Apple-tree': *trams*: vehicles for transporting coal underground.

mandrel: a miner's pick.

stalls: areas of coal-face allotted to particular groups of miners.

140 *concordance*: index of the Bible.

deacon: an elder of the Chapel congregation.

belly-bands: supports worn by miners to prevent ruptures.

141 'The Ambush': *Giovanni Bellini* was the son of Jacopo Bellini. His brother Gentile was also a painter. Giovanni lived from c. 1430–1516. Poets often write under the inspiration of paintings – cf. 'Musée Des Beaux Arts' by W. H. Auden.

imprecision: the snow falls irregularly on the ground.

142 'Cathedral Builders': *small beer*: weak beer.

clerestories: upper part of the nave of a church or cathedral, housing the upper windows.

'Salmon': *odyssey*: voyage (after Homer's *Odyssey*).

143 *rut*: mating.

144 *transilient*: leaping.

sickle-blades: shape of the leaping salmon.

in descant: above, higher than.

Diapasons: full volumes of sound.

shirred: puckered.

squanderous: abundant.

saraband: dance.

galactic: innumerable, like the stars of the Milky Way.

145 *Gautama*: the Buddha.

'The Key': *dotage*: old age.

Linus Yale: inventor of the lock.

146 *acrimony*: literally bitterness; he means the difficulty that the key had in unlocking the door.

litigants: literally people who have gone to law against one another. He means the key and the lock.

147 'Ancient Monuments': Wales has many standing stones, dolmens and other relics of prehistory. The poet first gives an impression of this richness and then shows, by his account of a dolmen in a field of barley, that these monuments are an integral part of the Welsh scene, they belong.

callow: literally inexperienced – compared with the age of the cultivated land the stones are very experienced.

elliptical: he is thinking of stone-circles.

accurate by the stars: the Bronze Age people who set up the stones were accurate astronomers.

scutched: cut.

Dolerite, *gabbro* and *porphyry* are all igneous rocks, the products of volcanic activity (*fired*). The Stonehenge bluestones are dolerite from Pembrokeshire.

solstice: solstices occur in summer and winter and are the times when the sun reaches its farthest point from the equator, 21 June and 21 December. Circles such as Stonehenge were used amongst other things to calculate these times.

cromlech: (or dolmen), a stone burial chamber of the Bronze Age, consisting of a large, flat stone (the capstone), supported on upright stones.

loquacious: literally talkative – he is trying to suggest the rustling sounds made by the wind-blown barley.

149   'Tricephalos': literally three-headed.

auguries: forecasts; prophecies.

Dannie Abse (b. 1923)

153   'Epithalamion' (marriage-song): an exuberant, youthful and witty poem, defying death through love and joy. Reminiscent in style of Dylan Thomas (*blackbird priests*, cf. *heron priested*).

154   'The Game': cf. 'The Ballad of Billy Rose' (p. 115).

the Swans: Swansea City F.C.

The Bluebirds: Cardiff City F.C.

Mephistopheles: devil who tempted Faustus to sell his soul.

eidetic: vividly clear.

155   *jugular*: literally to do with the neck – fans who were stretching their necks to watch, or shouting?

'Elegy for Dylan Thomas': Dylan Thomas died on 9 November 1953 in New York. Dannie Abse uses a Dylan-Thomas-like verse-form and style.

metronome: device for marking time. It ticks a regular beat.

156   'The French Master': *poison bottle*: usually dark green.

Lettres de mon Moulin: book by Alphonse Daudet (1840–97), literally *Letters from my Mill*. This book, often used in schools, is light, cheerful and poetic.

157   *Villon*: Francois Villon (1431–c. 63), poet, drunkard, libertine and criminal.

158   'As I Was Saying': Wordsworth (1770–1850); William Barnes (1801?–1886) wrote his poems in West Country dialect; John Clare (1793–1864) died in an asylum. All three are famous for their nature poetry.

159   'Return to Cardiff': *locus*: place, area.

mile wide Taff: as a child he thought the river very wide; as an adult he sees it in a different perspective.

certain news: that he was mortally ill.

Tiger Bay: dockland area of Cardiff, famous for its dangerous and exotic character. Now cleared away.

160   'Pathology of Colours': pathology is the study of diseases. As a doctor, Dannie Abse looks on colours in ways unusual in poetry.

tumour: cancerous growth.

hirsute: hairy; rough.

cathedral windows: the bright, stained-glass colours of the intestines.

bevelled: cut at a slant. Produces a prism-like effect.

'Car Journeys: 1. Down the M4': *disrobed*: literally undressed, here 'dead and buried'.

amateurs with gold sovereigns: it is often alleged that amateur Rugby players receive surreptitious payments.

Tawe: river. Swansea (Abertawe) stands at the mouth of the Tawe.

Patagonia: famous for its Welsh settlements.

161   *Ystalyfera*: industrial village in the upper Swansea Valley.

'A Night Out': *Auschwitz*: Nazi concentration camp where many Jews were killed in gas-chambers.

striped: prisoners wore striped clothing.

guttural: literally throaty. Refers to the grinding noises made by the wheels of the trucks.

chambers: gas-chambers. Victims were often deceived by being told that they were going for a shower.

au pair girl from Germany: wry irony – the speaker and his wife are, of course, Jewish.

162   'Moon Object': the *object* is a piece of moon-rock.

computer-speeches: speeches that sound as if made up by a computer because they are so predictable.

metal flag: the Americans used a special flag with metal supports to make it appear to fly on the moon.

The poet suggests that the scientist is disturbed and his way of thinking altered by this alien object.

163   'Three Street Musicians': *suicide notes*: a pun. The music is gloomy.

Raymond Garlick (b. 1926)

166   'Dylan Thomas at Tenby' is about one of the first readings of *Under Milk Wood*, given to a literary society at Tenby, Pembrokeshire, near the end of the poet's life.
the sleeping town: Llaregyb, the imaginary town of 'Milk Wood'.
eiderdown: a pun – eiderdowns used to be stuffed with the feathers of the Eider duck.
cantref: a 'hundred'; a division of land.

167   *October*: Dylan Thomas's birthday was in October. See 'Poem in October' (p. 69).
'Biographical Note': the poet gives a self-portrait, describing both his physical disability and his attitudes as a poet.
crown of thorn: pain, suffering.
to pin/A syntax on existence: to write poetry. An apt and epigrammatic description of the poet's art.
hustings: a platform from which speeches are made.

168   'Notes for a Picture': *morfa*: sea-marsh.
filigree: fine work in metal. He is suggesting the appearance of the shore with its lines and shapes.
runes: ancient writing consisting of lines and strokes. The poet suggests not only the appearance of the litter, but also a comment on its presence.
Eryri: Snowdonia.
aquatint: actually an engraving technique which gives soft light and shade effects; however, here the poet intended 'etching'.
Wyddfa: Yr Wyddfa is the Welsh name for Snowdon.

169   *verdigris*: green coating on copper.
'Winter Walk' is set in the Forest of Ommen, Holland; the walk is made frightening by the fear that wolves may have come down from the North because of the severity of the weather.

170   *chiaroscuro*: light and shade.

171   'Consider Kyffin': Morris Kyffin (c. 1555–98), an early Anglo-Welsh poet.
John Davies of Hereford (c. 1565–1618); Hugh Holland of Denbigh (1569–1633): both early Anglo-Welsh poets.
Lloyds and Llwyds, Vaughans: David Lloyd (1597–1663); Evan Lloyd (1734–76); David Lloyd (1752–1838); Morgan Llwyd (1619–59); Richard Llwyd (1752–1835); Sir William Vaughan (1577–1641); Henry Vaughan (1621–95): Anglo-Welsh writers

whom the poet regards as literary ancestors. For more information about them, read Raymond Garlick's *An Introduction to Anglo-Welsh Literature* (University of Wales Press 1970).

Samwell: David Samwell (1751–98) was surgeon on the 'Discovery'.

Poet Jones: John Jones of Llanasa (1788–1858).

David Hughes (fl. 1770–1817) author of *Poems by Hughes*.

172   'Fourth of May': 4 May is Remembrance Day in Holland, the day when Nazi Germany invaded in 1940. The poet hopes that Wales will never be similarly *crucified*.

173   'Personal Statement' may be compared with 'Biographical Note'.

raised in splints: links physical disability and the need for support with form in poetry.

tendril: (verb.). The lines support themselves on the frame like climbing plants.

sempiternal bines: everlasting stems.

espalier: artificial form of a tree with branches spread at right angles to the trunk for training on a wall or frame.

communicate/or else return: image from postal system where letters are often marked 'if undelivered return to . . .

174   *disparate*: different, unequal.

Very Light: a bright light used for signalling (a pun).

'Agincourt': battle fought in 1415 by Henry V against the French. The decisive force was the British bowmen, many of them Welsh.

Llansteffan: village at the mouth of the Tywy, 7 miles from Carmarthen. Raymond Garlick lives there.

bonemeal verdant: with flowers scattered over the ground.

175   *stakes*: formed a barricade to protect the infantry and archers from the charging French cavalry.

'A Touch of White' is about the serious illness of the poet's son and the effect of it upon his parents.

176   'Bilingualism': may be compared with 'Consider Kyffin' (p. 171). The poet is seeking a way in which Welsh and English may work together for the good of Wales. He feels that otherwise Wales will become a mere backwater and tourist playground.

Bibliography

LITERARY JOURNALS

Wales (ed. Keidrych Rhys) 1937–40, 1943–9, 1958–60.
The Welsh Review (ed. Gwyn Jones) 1939–48.
The Anglo-Welsh Review (ed. Roland Mathias). Dock Leaves Press 1949– .
Poetry Wales (ed. Sam Adams) Meic Stephens 1965–7, Christopher Davies 1967– .
Planet (ed. and published by Ned Thomas) 1970– .

ANTHOLOGIES

Griffiths, Bryn (ed.). *Welsh Voices, An Anthology of New Poetry from Wales.* Dent 1967.
Morgan, Gerald (ed.). *This World of Wales, An Anthology of Anglo-Welsh poetry from the 17th to the 20th Century.* University of Wales Press 1968.
Rhys, Keidrych (ed.). *Modern Welsh Poetry.* Faber & Faber 1944.
Williams, J. S. and Stephens, M. (eds.). *The Lilting House, An Anthology of Anglo-Welsh Poetry, 1917–1967.* Dent & C. Davies 1969.
Gwasg Gomer, Llandysul, publish annual anthologies of contemporary poetry. Available so far: *Poems '69* (ed. J. S. Williams); *Poems '70* (ed. F. Wyn Binding); *Poems '71* (ed. J. Hooker); *Poems '72* (ed. J. Ackerman); *Poems '73* (ed. G. Ramage).

GENERAL

Adams, Sam and Hughes, G. R. (eds.). *Triskel 1, Essays on Welsh and Anglo-Welsh Writers.* C. Davies 1971. *Triskel 2.* C. Davies 1973.
Garlick, Raymond. *An Introduction to Anglo-Welsh Literature. Writers of Wales.* University of Wales Press on behalf of the Welsh Arts Council 1970, reprinted 1972.

Jenkins, D. C. *Writing in 20th Century Wales, A Defence of the Anglo-Welsh*. Michigan 1955.

Jones, Glyn. *The Dragon has Two Tongues*. Dent 1968.

Jones, Gwyn. *The First Forty Years*. In *Triskel 1* (*see* Adams, Sam, above).

Lewis, Saunders. *Is There an Anglo-Welsh Literature?* University Registry, Cardiff 1939.

INDIVIDUAL POETS (titles of volumes of poetry and the names of publishers are given in the individual Introductions)

IDRIS DAVIES (1905–53)

Jenkins, Islwyn (ed. and introduced by R. George Thomas). *The Collected Poems of Idris Davies*. Gwasg Gomer 1972.

Jenkins, Islwyn. *Idris Davies. Writers of Wales*. University of Wales Press on behalf of the Welsh Arts Council 1972.

VERNON WATKINS (1906–67)

Mathias, Roland. 'A Note on Some Recent Poems by Vernon Watkins.' *Dock Leaves*, Vol. 1, no. 3, 1950.

Mathias, Roland. *Vernon Watkins. Writers of Wales*. University of Wales Press on behalf of the Welsh Arts Council 1974.

Norris, Leslie (ed.). *Vernon Watkins*. Faber & Faber 1969.

Norris, Leslie. 'Seeing Eternity: Vernon Watkins and the Poet's Task.' *Triskel 2*. C. Davies 1973.

Raine, Kathleen. 'Vernon Watkins, Poet of Tradition.' *Anglo-Welsh Review*, Vol. 14, no. 33, 1964.

Tributes to Vernon Watkins: *Anglo-Welsh Review*, Vol. 17, no. 39, 1968.

R. S. THOMAS (b. 1913)

Garlick, Raymond. Editorial. *Dock Leaves*, Vol. 6, no. 18, 1955.

Mathias, Roland. Editorial. *Anglo-Welsh Review*, Vol. 13, no. 31.

Merchant, W. M. 'R. S. Thomas.' *Critical Quarterly*, Vol. 2, no. 4, 1960.

Thomas, R. G. *R. S. Thomas. Writers and Their Work*. Longmans 1964.

Poetry Wales, Vol. 7, no. 4, 1972, is entirely devoted to R. S. Thomas.

DYLAN THOMAS (1914–53)

Jones, Daniel (ed.). *Dylan Thomas, The Poems*. Dent 1971.

Davies, Walford. *Dylan Thomas. Writers of Wales*. University of Wales Press on behalf of the Welsh Arts Council 1972.

Fitzgibbon, Constantine. *The Life of Dylan Thomas*. Dent 1965.

Fraser, G. S. *Dylan Thomas. Writers and Their Work*. Longmans 1957.

Holbrook, David. *Llareggub Revisited*. Bowes & Bowes 1962.

Jones, T. H. *Dylan Thomas. Writers and Critics*. Oliver & Boyd 1963.

Maud, R. N. *Entrances to Dylan Thomas's Poetry*. Scorpion Press 1963.

Tedlock, E. W. (ed.). *Dylan Thomas, The Legend and the Poet*.Thames & Hudson 1962.

ALUN LEWIS (1915–43)

John, Alun. *Alun Lewis. Writers of Wales*. University of Wales Press on behalf of the Welsh Arts Council 1970.

Williams, J. S. 'The Poetry of Alun Lewis'. *Anglo-Welsh Review*, Vol. 14, no. 33, 1964.

ROLAND MATHIAS (b. 1915)

Hooker, J. 'The Poetry of Roland Mathias'. *Poetry Wales*, Vol. 7, no. 1, 1971.

Mathias, Roland. *Artists in Wales*. Gwasg Gomer 1971.

HARRI WEBB (b. 1920)

Humfrey, Belinda. 'Harri Webb in "The Wrong Language"'. *Anglo-Welsh Review*, Vol. 21, no. 48, 1972.

Jenkins, W. Randal. 'Review of *The Green Desert*'. *Anglo-Welsh Review*, Vol. 19, no. 43, 1970.

LESLIE NORRIS (b. 1921)

Adams, Sam. 'The Poetry of Leslie Norris'. *Poetry Wales*, Vol. 7, no. 2, 1971.

Jenkins, W. Randal. 'The Poetry of Leslie Norris'. *Anglo-Welsh Review*, Vol. 20, no. 46, 1972.

HARRI JONES (1921–65)

Jones, Gwyn. *Poetry Wales*, Vol. 1, 1965.

Partridge, O. J. 'The Verse of T. H. Jones'. *Poetry Wales*, Vol. 1, no. 2, 1965.

A volume in the *Writers of Wales* series has been commissioned.

JOHN ORMOND (b. 1923)

Jenkins, W. Randal. 'The Poetry of John Ormond'. *Poetry Wales*, Vol. 8, no. 1, 1972.
Ormond, John. *Artists in Wales II*. Gwasg Gomer 1973.

DANNIE ABSE (b. 1923)

Mathias, Roland. 'The Poetry of Dannie Abse I'. *Anglo-Welsh Review*, Vol. 15, no. 36, 1966.
Mathias, Roland. 'The Poetry of Dannie Abse II'. *Anglo-Welsh Review*, Vol. 16, no. 38, 1967.

RAYMOND GARLICK (b. 1926)

Hill, J. 'The Poetry of Raymond Garlick'. *Anglo-Welsh Review*, Vol. 21, no. 47, 1972.
Garlick, Raymond. *Artists in Wales II*. Gwasg Gomer 1973.

GRAMOPHONE RECORDS

Dannie Abse (& Leslie Norris) reading their poems. Argo PLP 1155.
Idris Davies. Poetry and Prose (ed. Islwyn Jenkins). Argo ZPL 1181.
Raymond Garlick (& John Ormond) reading their work. Argo PLP 1156.
Leslie Norris (& Dannie Abse) reading their work. Argo PLP 1155.
John Ormond (& Raymond Garlick) reading their work. Argo PLP 1156.
Dylan Thomas. Under Milk Wood. Caedmon TC 0996/7. Argo RG 21/2.
　　　　　　　　Reading his poems, Vol. 1. Caedmon TC 1002.
　　　　　　　　　　　　Vol. 2. Caedmon TC 1018.
　　　　　　　　　　　　Vol. 3. Caedmon TC 1043.
　　　　　　　　　　　　Vol. 4. Caedmon TC 1061.
　　　　　　Poems read by Richard Burton. Argo RG 43.
Harri Webb. *The Green Desert (Poetry, Ballads, Songs)*. Cambrian CLP 603.
The records of poetry by Dannie Abse, Idris Davies, Raymond Garlick, Leslie Norris and John Ormond are made by Argo on behalf of the Welsh Arts Council.

BIBLIOGRAPHIES

Jones, Brynmor *A Bibliography of Anglo-Welsh Literature 1900–1965*. Wales & Monmouthshire Library Association 1970.
Stephens, Meic *A Reader's Guide to Wales*. National Book League 1973.

INDEX OF FIRST LINES